BARONESSA GELATERIA
in Boston's North End

In addition to our regular flavors of
Italian gelato, this month we are featuring:

- **Espresso laced with Irish Cream**

  Shane was proud of his heritage as a
  firefighter in his Irish immigrant family. He
  approached his work the same way he did
  his life—fearlessly. That is, until he found
  himself unsettled by the feelings he had for
  Emily Barone....

- **Angel food cake**

  Whether Shane's kiss was her first, Emily
  didn't remember. She did know it was the
  only one that mattered. When he took her in
  his arms, her virgin heart had never beat so
  fast, never yearned so much....

- **Cherries flambé, made and lit at your
  table**

  Despite their differences, Shane could not
  douse his desires, nor could Emily deny her
  burning need to be with him. Their passion
  threatened to blaze out of control—hot and
  dangerous....

  Buon appetito!

Dear Reader,

Let Silhouette Desire rejuvenate your romantic spirit in May with six new passionate, powerful and provocative love stories.

Our compelling yearlong twelve-book series DYNASTIES: TH BARONES continues with *Where There's Smoke…* (#1507) by Barbara McCauley, in which a fireman as courageous as he is gorgeous saves the life and wins the heart of a Barone heiress. Next, a domineering cowboy clashes with a mysterious woman hiding on his ranch, in *The Gentrys: Cinco* (#1508), the launch title of THE GENTRYS, a new three-book miniseries by Linda Conrad.

A night of passion brings new love to a rancher who lost his family and his leg in a tragic accident in *Cherokee Baby* (#1509) by reader favorite Sheri WhiteFeather. *Sleeping with Beauty* (#1510) by Laura Wright features a sheltered princess who slips past the defenses of a love-shy U.S. Marshal. A dynamic Texan inspires a sperm-bank-bound thirtysomething stranger to try conceiving the old-fashioned way in *The Cowboy's Baby Bargain* (#1511) by Emilie Rose, the latest title in Desire's BABY BANK theme promotion. And in *Her Convenient Millionaire* (#1512) by Gail Dayton, a pretend marriage between a Palm Beach socialite and her millionaire beau turns into real passion.

Why miss even one of these brand-new, red-hot love stories? Get all six and share in the excitement from Silhouette Desire this month.

Enjoy!

Melissa Jeglinski
Senior Editor, Silhouette Desire

Please address questions and book requests to:
Silhouette Reader Service
U.S.: 3010 Walden Ave., P.O. Box 1325, Buffalo, NY 14269
Canadian: P.O. Box 609, Fort Erie, Ont. L2A 5X3

Where There's Smoke...

BARBARA McCAULEY

Published by Silhouette Books
America's Publisher of Contemporary Romance

If you purchased this book without a cover you should be aware
that this book is stolen property. It was reported as "unsold and
destroyed" to the publisher, and neither the author nor the
publisher has received any payment for this "stripped book."

Special thanks and acknowledgment are given to
Barbara McCauley for her contribution
to the DYNASTIES: THE BARONES series.

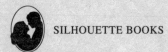 SILHOUETTE BOOKS

ISBN 0-373-76507-X

WHERE THERE'S SMOKE…

Copyright © 2003 by Harlequin Books S.A.

All rights reserved. Except for use in any review, the reproduction
or utilization of this work in whole or in part in any form by any
electronic, mechanical or other means, now known or hereafter
invented, including xerography, photocopying and recording, or in
any information storage or retrieval system, is forbidden without
the written permission of the editorial office, Silhouette Books,
233 Broadway, New York, NY 10279 U.S.A.

All characters in this book have no existence outside the imagination of
the author and have no relation whatsoever to anyone bearing the same
name or names. They are not even distantly inspired by any individual
known or unknown to the author, and all incidents are pure invention.

This edition published by arrangement with Harlequin Books S.A.

® and TM are trademarks of Harlequin Books S.A., used under license.
Trademarks indicated with ® are registered in the United States Patent
and Trademark Office, the Canadian Trade Marks Office and in other
countries.

Visit Silhouette at www.eHarlequin.com

Printed in U.S.A.

Books by Barbara McCauley

Silhouette Desire

Woman Tamer #621
Man from Cougar Pass #698
Her Kind of Man #771
Whitehorn's Woman #803
A Man Like Cade #832
Nightfire #875
*Texas Heat #917
*Texas Temptation #948
*Texas Pride #971
Midnight Bride #1028
The Nanny and the Reluctant Rancher #1066
Courtship in Granite Ridge #1128
Seduction of the Reluctant Bride #1144
†Blackhawk's Sweet Revenge #1230
†Secret Baby Santos #1236
†Killian's Passion #1242
†Callan's Proposition #1290
†Reese's Wild Wager #1360
Fortune's Secret Daughter #1390
†Sinclair's Surprise Baby #1402
†Taming Blackhawk #1437
†In Blackhawk's Bed #1447
Royally Pregnant #1480
†That Blackhawk Bride #1491
Where There's Smoke... #1507

Silhouette Intimate Moments

†Gabriel's Honor #1024

*Hearts of Stone
†Secrets!

BARBARA McCAULEY,

who has written more than twenty novels for Silhouette Books, lives in Southern California with her own handsome hero husband, Frank, who makes it easy to believe in and write about the magic of romance. Barbara's stories have won and been nominated for numerous awards, including the prestigious RITA® Award from the Romance Writers of America, Best Desire of the Year from *Romantic Times* and Best Short Contemporary from the National Reader's Choice Awards.

DYNASTIES:
THE
BARONES

Meet the Barones of Boston—
an elite clan caught in a web of danger, deceit…and desire!

Shane Cummings—He has no attachments, no
commitments. Even his sailboat home isn't grounded.
This firefighter's a loner who lives life for today—
and he wants to keep it that way.…

Emily Barone—She personifies stability. Warm and secure
in her big, loving family, she's got the powerful Barones
behind her. Emily wants permanence—at least she would
if she could remember who she was.…

Derrick Barone—He looks out for Emily, as older brothers
do. But does he have only her best interests at heart?

intended to sell secret recipes from the family gelato business to a rival company.

He'd been careful not to raise suspicion, Emily knew. Even as Derrick's secretary, Emily might not have ever noticed anything amiss if earlier today she hadn't accidentally overheard a few whispered words of a phone call on his private line, words that had made her uneasy. When he'd left his office a few minutes later, she'd gone in and pushed redial, only to hear a receptionist for Snowcream, Inc., Baronessa Gelati's biggest competitor, answer the phone.

She'd had to wait until the plant had closed this evening and everyone left before she could search for evidence to confirm Derrick's betrayal. It had taken her nearly an hour to jimmy the lock on his desk, another fifteen minutes to find the file containing detailed notes from his conversation with Grant Summers, CEO of Snowcream. The file also contained dates and times Derrick had met with Summers, listed the amount of money to be exchanged for the information and the Swiss bank account the money would be transferred into.

Emily swallowed the lump in her throat and blinked back her tears. She knew she was naive. At twenty-four, she still tried to see the good in people, still hoped that in the end a person would do the right thing. She'd prayed she'd been wrong about Derrick, hadn't wanted to believe that her own brother would steal from anyone, let alone Baronessa Gelati.

She was glad her father, Paul Barone, had chosen to become a lawyer rather than go into the business Grandfather Marco had started over a half century ago. Just the thought of taking this damning information to her parents made Emily sick to her stomach. It would kill her mother to learn that her son was capable of such a betrayal.

But it was possible her parents might never have to know, Emily thought as she turned off the copy machine. Her father's brother, Carlo, ran Baronessa. She knew she couldn't look the other way, that she had to take this evidence to her uncle. She knew he would have a solution that would quietly remove Derrick from his position as VP of Quality Assurance Department and possibly even cover up any potential scandal to the company or the family.

Uncle Carlo would know what to do; Emily was certain of it. With his booming, deep voice, he was a little intimidating at times, but he was a good man, a fair man who loved his wife and children and was fiercely protective of the entire family.

At the sound of a door closing in an outer office, Emily froze. Quickly she reached across to the single table lamp she'd turned on when she came in. She stood in the dark, listening, heard a quiet shuffling sound, then nothing. Slowly she moved toward the closed blinds over the small copy-room window and peeked out through the side. She'd left the outer lights off, but she could see the outline of a tall, thin man at one of the desks.

She gasped as the man turned. Dear God! It was Derrick!

When he glanced in her direction, Emily jumped back. She'd never been a good liar. If he found her here, she knew she'd never be able to talk her way out of this mess. He'd only have to look at her face to know what she'd discovered, and he'd be furious. She couldn't confront him yet, not until she talked to Uncle Carlo.

Pressing her back to the wall, she waited, then finally heard the outer door close. Slowly she released the breath she'd been holding. To be sure he'd left the plant, she'd wait a while before she came out. She could take no chances that he might return and find her putting the file back in his desk, or discover her on her way out with the copies she'd made.

After several minutes, there were still no sounds, except for the soft ticking of the copy-room wall clock and the beating of her own heart. The office was quiet. Thank goodness. She breathed a sigh of relief. She'd wait two more minutes and—

Once again she froze. And sniffed.

Smoke?

She flipped on the lamp again and glanced down. Thin ribbons of wispy gray smoke curled up from underneath the door.

Oh God, no...

She shoved the blinds apart and looked out. Flames shot up from the middle of the office and were spreading quickly across the room.

Why hadn't the alarm gone off? And why hadn't the sprinklers come on? Unless Derrick—

No! She couldn't believe that he would do such a terrible thing. Selling secret formulas was one thing, but arson was another. He couldn't—*wouldn't*—commit such a heinous crime.

She grabbed her purse and both files. There'd be

no time to replace the original back into Derrick's desk, but she couldn't think about that now. She had to get out quickly, before the fire completely engulfed the office. Since there was no window to the outside from the copy room, she had no choice but to make a dash across the outer office and hopefully skirt the flames. If she could get to the windows overlooking the street two stories below, she could attract someone's attention. If worse came to worst—and she prayed it wouldn't—she would have to jump.

She gulped in air, then threw open the door and ran. A blast of heat made her stumble, but she recovered and kept going. In the distance she heard the wail of sirens and the sound gave her hope. They're coming, she thought as the wail and the deep sound of horns grew louder. They're almost here.

The fire crackled around her, sparks flew, singeing her face and bare legs. The smoke burned her throat and her eyes. But she made it to the window, was reaching for the handle when the sound of a loud crack from behind her made her whip her head around. She watched in horror as the heavy steel bindings that supported the dropped ceiling gave way. Like a giant zipper opening, the ceiling ripped apart, raining metal and plaster tiles. Frantic, Emily turned back to the window, but the crack overhead rushed toward her like a hideous, furious monster.

Helpless to stop it, she went down.

"This is Hemming Taylor from KLRT." The pretty blond reporter held the microphone close as she spoke to the television cameraman. "First on the scene and reporting to you live from Brookline, Massachusetts, where behind me a fire rages inside one of the buildings that make up the Baronessa Gelati manufacturing plant. It appears that flames have already consumed the third floor of the plant's main offices, and as you can see—'' Hemming pointed with one hand and the camera swept up to catch a full shot of the building ''—the fire seems to have spread to the second floor, as well. Firefighters already on the scene are working valiantly to douse the flames, and an unconfirmed report of a woman inside the building has heightened the tension among the firefighters and onlookers alike. We're told that the call came in approximately ten minutes ago and—''

An explosion from the third floor had the reporter and crew running for cover. Car alarms blared from the streets, and firefighters working outside the building dropped to protect themselves from flying debris.

Inside the building, in the smoke-filled stairwell between the first and second floors, the blast from overhead threw Shane Cummings to his knees. He recovered quickly, stood and glanced back at his partner, Matt.

''You okay?'' Shane yelled over a second, smaller explosion.

Matt lifted a hand, gave Shane the go-ahead sign, then pointed to the door leading to the second story.

As a unit, Shane and Matt moved up the stairwell. Shane knew they were quickly running out of time, that they should get out now, but the security guard working the building across the street had insisted he saw a woman in a second-story window that faced the street. Two minutes, Shane told himself as he kicked the door open with his boot. Two minutes and they were out of here.

"We've entered the second story from the stairwell." Shane had to yell into his radio headset over the crackle of flames and crashing debris. "The room is approximately forty by fifty, charged with heavy smoke, the ceiling is down. Female reported at east window and we're heading there now."

"Negative, Cummings." Chief Griffin's raspy voice crackled over the radio. "The third floor is engulfed. Get your butts out of there now."

"Five minutes." Shane glanced back at Matt, who nodded. "Then we're outta here pronto."

"No heroics, Cummings," Griffin barked. "That's a command, dammit. Get your ass out of there *now*."

"Two minutes," Shane negotiated. "Get a ladder at the window and we'll come through there."

While Chief Griffin erupted into a litany of expletives and threats, Shane hunkered down under the cloud of smoke and pressed forward. Matt moved with him.

Adrenaline pumped through Shane's blood as he edged around a wall of flames, then spotted the windows across the rows of desks in the office. Between the rubble and the smoke, it was impossible to see if anyone was lying on the floor. He made his way across the room, then spotted a pair of long, bare legs protruding from under a pile of ceiling tiles.

"Found her," Shane yelled back to Matt, then spoke into his headset again. "This is Cummings. I've located the female approximately six feet from the east window. She may be unconscious. Do you copy?''

The hiss of static came back, then Griffin said, ''We copy, Cummings. Get her and get the hell out of there.''

''My plan exactly. Over.''

Dropping to the pile of rubble on the floor, he pitched broken tiles and chunks of plaster until he finally uncovered the woman's still body.

She was young, probably early twenties, Shane noted as he scooped her up into his arms, and he doubted she tipped the scales past a hundred pounds. Though dust and soot covered her, he saw no evidence of burns on her clothes or her bare arms and legs.

When he stood, her hair fell away from her face and her eyelids fluttered open. He saw the confusion and fear in her eyes as she looked up at him.

''I've got you,'' he yelled. ''Is there anyone else in here?''

He couldn't hear what she said, but he hoped like hell her answer was no. Another explosion from somewhere overhead made him stumble backward. Shane gritted his teeth and held the woman close while debris rained down on them. She buried her head against his chest.

''We have to go out through the window,'' he yelled over the thunderous roar of the fire. ''Can you hang on?''

She nodded, then slid her arms up and circled his neck tightly.

Holding the woman in his arms, Shane stepped to

the window and opened it, felt his own lungs burn
from the cloud of smoke that poured out into the crisp
night air. He heard the din of men and women working below, saw the flash of red lights spinning from
the trucks. There were shouts, then the ladder appeared.

"Here we go." Shane shifted the woman to one
arm so the upper part of her body draped over his
shoulder. He held her tight, then backed out of the
window. Matt was right behind him.

Shane had barely stepped off the ladder when another explosion blasted through the second story,
blowing out the windows. He dropped to the ground,
shielding the woman's body with his own. She shuddered against him, held tightly to his jacket while
glass and pieces of brick crashed down on them.

Shane quickly glanced behind him to make sure
Matt was all right, then breathed a sigh of relief at
the sight of his partner picking himself up off the
sidewalk and giving him a thumbs-up.

None too gently, Shane scooped the woman back
up into his arms and made a dash to the waiting paramedics, who slid her onto a gurney and slipped an
oxygen mask over her face. As they carried her away,
Shane watched the woman lift her head and hold his
gaze. She looked so small lying there, shivering. The
sight of blood trickling down her soot-smudged forehead made Shane's stomach constrict. He started to
follow her, but was stopped short at the sound of
Chief Griffin's bellow.

"Cummings!"

Griffin, five foot ten and built like a bull, came

charging at him. "I told you to get the hell out of there," the chief roared. "I oughta suspend your ass for such a stupid stunt."

Shane removed his helmet and wiped the sweat on his brow. "I didn't have a—"

"Save it," Griffin barked. "You're bleeding, dammit. Go with the ambulance, then get your butt back to the station to file a report."

"Yes, sir."

The camera crews had already converged on the ambulance like spring locusts. Ignoring the microphones shoved in his face, Shane pushed his way through the crowd and climbed into the ambulance. The woman seemed to relax when he sat beside her. When he covered her slender fingers with his own and smiled down at her, she smiled weakly back, then closed her eyes and slipped into unconsciousness.

Five seconds later, with the siren wailing and the lights flashing, they were headed for Brookline Hospital.

"Emily...Emily..."

The distant sound of a man's voice pulled her out of the thick blanket of fog surrounding her, worsened the ache in her head and the burning in her chest. She felt as if she were floating somewhere, disembodied....

"Emily, can you hear me?"

Go away, she wanted to say, but couldn't make her mouth move. Couldn't make any part of her body move. She heard the ring of a telephone...a man calling for a nurse…the *squish-squish-squish* of rubber soles on a tile floor.

Where am I? she wondered. And why did she smell smoke? Smoke and antiseptic…and a man's cologne?

"Emily, wake up. It's Derrick."

Derrick? She didn't know anyone named Derrick. But the voice was closer now, persistent. She tried to open her eyes, but they were so heavy and she was so tired. She didn't know who Emily was and she didn't care. She just wanted to sleep.

"I called Mom and Dad," the man said, "but they're at the opera and I had to leave a message. Emily, for God's sake, open your eyes and talk to me."

I don't want to talk, she thought, and rolled her head away. The sheets underneath her were cool and crisp, the blanket covering her soft and warm. *She* felt soft and warm, she realized. And sleepy. So very sleepy…

"What were you doing at the plant?" The man's voice turned to a harsh whisper. "You'd already left before me, why did you go back?"

She had no idea who was speaking to her or what he was talking about. She felt the moan vibrate deep in her throat, then the pounding in her head increased.

Slowly she opened her eyes, saw the blurred outline of a man standing over her. He was tall and thin, his hair and eyes dark brown. She blinked against the light and the pain, watched the image take shape. His features were sharp, his mouth pressed into a thin line. The black suit he wore was tailored, his tie a shim-

mering silver against his white dress shirt. The strong
spicy scent of his cologne made her cough.

He leaned in closer and took her hand in his. She
wanted to pull away but hadn't the strength.

"Talk to me," he said, still keeping his voice low.
"Tell me why you were at the plant."

I'm in a hospital, she realized as she saw the tube
running from her arm up to the hanging IV bag beside
her bed. "I—" She drew in a slow, painful breath.
"I don't know."

His hand tightened on hers. "What do you mean,
you don't know? How can you not know?"

I don't know how I don't know, she tried to say,
but her lungs were burning and her brain felt as if
there were shards of glass tumbling inside. She struggled to keep her eyes open and focused on the man
questioning her, struggled to keep her thoughts from
bumping into one another. Derrick. He'd said his
name was Derrick.

"You left the plant thirty minutes before me." He
narrowed his gaze. "I watched you drive away. What
were you doing there?"

"I...don't know...what you're talking about," she
managed to say, but the words cost her and she started
to cough again.

"Dammit, Emily, what are you—"

A knock at the half-open door stopped him. With
a frown, Derrick straightened. "What is it?"

"I came to check on Emily."

That voice. Deep, a bit hoarse. So familiar, she
thought. So comforting. Though her eyelids were
heavy, she lifted her gaze toward the doorway.

"Who are you?" Derrick demanded.

"A friend." The man wore faded jeans, a denim jacket and black boots. His gaze flicked over Derrick as he moved into the room. "Who are you?"

"Derrick Barone." Derrick stood and squared his shoulders. "Emily's brother."

Emily felt her pulse skip as the man moved closer to her bed. She knew him, she was certain she did. She just didn't know *how*.

He was tall, close to six feet, his chest broad and upper arms solid muscle. His sandy-brown hair was short and neat on the sides, just long enough on top to allow several thick strands to dip down in the middle of his forehead. His eyes were green—no, blue. Both, she finally decided, and held her breath as he turned his incredible gaze on her.

"How you feeling?" he asked her.

Before she could attempt an answer, Derrick stepped forward. "Excuse me. I didn't catch your name."

"Shane." He kept his eyes on Emily. "Shane Cummings."

"I know most of my sister's friends," Derrick said. "I don't believe we've met."

"We haven't." Shane moved around Derrick and came closer to the bed. "Hey, Cinderella, how you doing?"

Cinderella? Why would he call her that? she wondered. She doubted she'd left any glass slippers behind or—

Pain seized her, shot like an arrow through her

temple, had her gasping for breath and squeezing her eyes shut.

Fire...flames everywhere...smoke...

The sounds came back to her. The crackling heat, an explosion, shattering glass.

She reached out, felt the comfort of Shane's large hand closing over her own.

I've got you....

She heard Shane's voice, felt his arms lifting her out of the ashes and rubble. He'd carried her down a ladder, covered her body with his to protect her. Stayed with her.

That was all she could remember. Nothing before that moment he'd scooped her up in his arms, nothing after he'd climbed into the ambulance with her.

As the pain eased, she opened her eyes and saw the concern in his furrowed brow.

"Shall I get the doctor?" he asked quietly.

"Now, see here." Derrick smoothed a hand down his tie. "I don't know who you are, or why you're here, but my sister's been through a terrible ordeal. I would appreciate it if you would—"

"Mr. Barone?" A redheaded nurse stuck her head in the door. "Your parents are on the phone at the desk. They asked to speak with you."

Derrick glanced at Shane, then Emily. "I'll be right back. If you need anything—"

"I'll be here," Shane said evenly.

Derrick frowned, then followed the nurse.

"You...saved me," Emily murmured.

"You mean just now, or earlier?"

"Both."

He smiled down at her. "Do you remember me?"

"The fire… You carried me out.…"

When she started to cough, he squeezed her hand. "The doc says you're going to be fine, but you've sucked some smoke into your lungs, which is going to make them burn for a day or two. And since a ceiling came down on your head, I suspect that's gotta hurt, too."

She nodded, then reached up and touched the bandage taped high on her temple. "What happened?"

"We were hoping you might be able to tell us. You were the only person in the building when it caught fire."

"Building?"

"Baronessa Gelati." When she did not respond to the name, Shane lifted a brow. "Where you work."

She closed her eyes, felt the pounding in her brain start up with renewed vigor. Why couldn't she remember?

"Mr. Cummings." A blond woman wearing a white doctor's coat and black skirt came into the room. "I believe I sent you home."

"I was on my way, Doc." His expression innocent, Shane stuck his hands into his front pockets and stepped away from the bed. "But when I saw Miss Barone was conscious, I thought she might be able to tell us how the fire started."

The doctor threw a dubious glance at Shane, pushed her black-rimmed glasses up her nose, then looked at Emily. "I'm Dr. Tuscano. How's that head of yours feeling?"

"Like it's trying to hatch," Emily said weakly.

The doctor smiled. "I had to give you a few stitches along your hairline, but they should heal without a noticeable scar. We're giving you pain medication in your IV right now, but if you do well through the rest of the night, we'll take you off in the morning. Other than the laceration on your head, some bumps and bruises and a little smoke in your lungs, you're in great shape considering your ordeal."

"Shane saved my life," Emily whispered.

"I believe he did," Dr. Tuscano agreed as she made a note in Emily's chart. "Your family will be very happy to hear you'll be all right."

"My family?"

The doctor paused in her writing and glanced up. Frowning, she set her chart down and pulled a small flashlight out of her pocket. "You don't remember the accident?"

"No." Emily winced at the light the doctor shone in her eyes.

"Do you know who you are, where you live?"

Who she was? The pain in her head spiraled. She gathered from the conversation her name was Emily Barone. But she didn't know who she really was. Nor where she lived. "No."

"Hmm. A mild concussion, but nothing severe." Dr. Tuscano slipped the flashlight back into her coat pocket and picked up the chart again. "Except for your parents, who are on their way here now, you should have no more visitors."

"Dr. Tuscano—" the redheaded nurse stuck her head back in the doorway "—you're wanted on line three. Dr. Heaton."

"Be right there." Smiling, the doctor patted Emily's hand. "I'll be here in the morning to check on you. We'll see how you feel after a good night's rest."

Emily watched the doctor leave, then slowly turned her head toward Shane. He stood at the foot of her bed, his hands still in his pockets. She saw the worry in his gaze, had the strangest desire to touch his cheek, to comfort as much as to be comforted.

"I better go," he said after a long moment. "I just wanted to make sure you were all right."

But she wasn't all right. She didn't know who she was, or what had happened to her; she had stitches in her head and an IV stuck in her arm.

She felt like a child. Alone and frightened. The only person she knew, the only person she could remember, was Shane. She didn't want him to leave. She knew if he were here that she would be all right, that she could go to sleep and nothing would happen to her.

"Thank you for coming." She silently cursed the tears burning her eyes.

"What's wrong?" Frowning, he moved closer. "Are you in pain? Should I call the doctor?"

"No." She turned her head away. "I'm sorry. It's silly."

"What's silly?"

"I thought maybe…if you wouldn't mind…"

"What?"

"Could you…" She turned her head back to face him. "Could you stay with me, just until I fall asleep?"

He stared at her for a long moment, then nodded and reached for a chair and sat. "Yeah," he said with a smile. "I could do that."

"Thank you."

She knew he was watching her, but it didn't make her feel self-conscious. It made her feel safe.

She welcomed sleep, was certain that when she woke, her world would make sense again. That she would remember. Her eyelids grew heavy, and with a soft sigh she let the darkness wash over her.

Two

In the spring, tourists came to Boston Harbor Marina in droves. Wearing their hats and sunscreen and fancy digital cameras with long-distance lens, families of sightseers converged on the docks. While dads clicked away, moms held on tightly to impatient little hands more eager to test the water rather than look at it. They ate foot-long hot dogs from Arnie's Dog Cart at the end of the pier, ice cream cones from a vendor nicknamed Marty the Mariner, who entertained his clientele with stories of mermaids and ghost ships, then they took a two-hour tour of Boston Harbor.

From the deck of his sailboat, Shane watched the first tour bus of the day pull into a parking lot on the other side of the marina. A great place to visit, he thought, taking a long sip from the mug of steaming black coffee in his hand.

An even better place to live.

Half the year he lived in an apartment over his uncle's pub, the other half he lived here in the marina. He'd used the money from his mom's life insurance policy to buy the *Free Spirit,* a thirty-six-foot single-mast sloop. Marjorie Cummings had loved the ocean, had enjoyed the sailing trips her son had taken her on before and even after she'd fallen ill. Shane liked to think that he'd made her smile when he'd bought the boat and moved in.

Damn, but he missed that smile.

The sound of a powerboat pulling away from its slip caught his attention, and he lifted a hand in greeting as *The Sea Breeze* passed by. She was a pretty little yacht. Built for show as well as speed. And while Shane admired the shiny chrome and custom paint, the fancy boat with all its bells and whistles and oversize stateroom was simply not his style. What would he do with all that space? he thought in amusement. He didn't even have a girlfriend, let alone a wife, though a few of the women he'd dated had made it clear they'd be happy to change his marital status.

But he was content with his life just the way it was. He came and went as he pleased, sometimes for days at a time. Other than his uncle, Shane had no one to answer to. No one checking up on him, wondering where he was, whom he was with or what he was doing. And that was fine with him.

He glanced up at a pair of seagulls flapping noisily overhead, screeching at each other in argument over a chunk of bread scavenged from a nearby trash can.

The damp, salty air was crisp and cool, but the early morning fog had already begun to lift and the weather promised to be clear and warm. A good day for sailing, he mused, briefly considered taking the boat out, then decided against it. He'd promised his uncle he'd come by and help out with the lunch crowd, and he still needed to revarnish the last section of deck he'd been sanding for the past few days. He had plenty to do to keep his hands and mind occupied.

So why, then, had he spent most of last night and this morning thinking about a pretty brunette with velvet-brown eyes and a wide, luscious mouth that would tempt a monk?

After he'd been booted out of Emily's room last night, Shane had gone home, poured himself a cold beer, then sat on the deck of his boat in the darkness and sifted through what he'd learned about Emily Barone from the nurses.

The Barone family and their gelato empire, Baronessa Gelati, had been in the papers quite a bit lately, he'd been told. Tabloid stuff, most of it revolving around some rather risqué photographs of one of Emily's cousins taken with a Baronessa public relations man, and something about a batch of gelato that had been tainted with habaneros. He'd also learned that Emily had an older sister and two older twin brothers, one of whom he'd met last night and instantly disliked. When he'd walked in and found Derrick bullying Emily, it had been all Shane could do not to grab the jerk by the scruff of his neck and throw him out on his butt. Fortunately, the nurse had interrupted with the phone call, then the doctor had banned all visitors.

Still, Shane had been restless all night, had felt uneasy knowing that Emily might wake and still not know who she was or what had happened to her. He knew, of course, that her parents would be there, that she'd be well cared for. But strangely, it didn't ease his concern.

Shane scrubbed a hand over his face, then tossed back the rest of his coffee. He had no business thinking about Emily, wondering what was going to happen to her. He'd simply done his job by pulling her out of the burning building. Her injuries weren't life-threatening. She had her family to take care of her now.

She'd be fine, he told himself with a shrug. Emily Barone wasn't his concern any longer, and she most certainly wasn't his problem.

"Emily, can I get you something, dear? Some water, or another pillow?"

Emily glanced at the woman sitting beside her bed. Her hair was a soft blond, the style short and chic, her eyes pale blue with fine webs of wrinkles in the corners. She was still dressed in the sleek black suit she'd worn to the opera the evening before, but she looked as though she'd just stepped out of a limousine. The single strand of pearls resting at the base of her slender neck suited her porcelain skin, Emily thought. She was tall and elegant, and quite beautiful.

The woman was her mother, Emily knew, but there was nothing remotely familiar about her.

"I'm fine, thank you," Emily said. "Really."

"Exactly what she told you five minutes ago when you asked," a man said as he turned from the window where he'd been quietly standing. "Let her rest, Sandra. Let her think."

The man who spoke was her father, Paul Barone. For a man, he wasn't tall, maybe around five nine, but he was stocky, with a thick chest and neck. If her mother hadn't told her that he was a lawyer, Emily would have guessed him to be a well-tailored bouncer. His hair was dark and thinning, his brows low and thick over deep brown eyes. He'd barely said more than a dozen words since they'd arrived, had preferred to let his wife do the talking while he took everything in.

There'd been a battery of tests when Emily had awakened this morning. A brain scan, more blood work, blood pressure. Dozens of questions about her past that she hadn't been able to answer. Dr. Tuscano had been thorough with her prodding and probing, and had pronounced her patient to be in excellent health. Except for one little thing.

Amnesia.

It had taken quite some time to digest the word. It was one thing to know what it meant, Emily thought, to know that such a thing existed, and quite another to *live* it.

Dr. Tuscano had reassured Emily and her parents that a loss of memory following a head trauma was nothing to worry about. Plus there was the emotional trauma to consider, as well, the doctor had said. Though no one knew exactly what had happened, it was reasonable to presume that Emily had been terrified, running to escape the flames and smoke when the ceiling had collapsed.

When—or if—her memory would return remained to be seen.

A young man brought a huge bouquet of brightly colored flowers into the room, the second bouquet she'd received this morning. Her mother accepted them, then looked at the card.

"They're from Claudia," Sandra said and glanced at her watch. "She was in a meeting in Washington, D.C., but caught the first plane out this morning when we called. She's worried sick about you, and Daniel is, too, of course. He's driving down from Manchester now. It took me forever to reach him, but then, you know how he is."

No, she *didn't* know how he was. She didn't know him at all, or anyone else. She'd been told she had a sister named Claudia and a brother named Daniel— Derrick's twin—but she didn't *know* them. And the thought of all these people coming to see her, asking her questions, trying to make her remember, made her head start to pound again.

Emily closed her eyes and thought of Shane. He was her only connection, the only familiar person in what felt like a foreign land. He'd stayed with her last night until she'd fallen asleep. She knew it was silly of her, but she'd wished he'd been there when she'd woken this morning.

The thought that she probably wouldn't see him again made her chest ache.

"I've said something wrong," Sandra said. "I'm

so sorry. I—I'm a little tired and seeing you lying here like this, knowing that you almost—'' Sandra's voice faltered, then she sucked in a breath and blinked back the threatening tears. "I just love you so much."

"Thank you." Though she couldn't return the sentiment, Emily reached for her mother's hand. "It's nice to know I have a family, people who care about me. Why don't you and…Dad go home and rest. Come back this afternoon."

"I can't leave you like this, all alone, not knowing—''

"Sandra." Paul Barone moved beside his wife and put a hand on her shoulder. "Emily needs to rest, too. She can't do that with us hovering. We'll come back later."

"I suppose you're right." But there was still reluctance in Sandra's tired eyes. "We do need to shower and change. Lord knows, these heels are killing my feet."

"I'll be fine." Emily forced a smile. "Really."

With a sigh, Sandra leaned forward and kissed her daughter's cheek. "If you need anything, just call the house. We can be back here in twenty minutes. I'll leave instructions with Annie to wake me if I'm sleeping. Don't worry about—''

"Sandra, enough." Paul took his wife's arm, then bent and gave Emily a peck on her forehead. "We'll be back in a few hours. Sleep. You'll need your strength when the rest of the troop gets here."

Alone, Emily released the breath she'd been holding. The crescendo of pain in her temple had risen from a slow, irregular pulse to a steady, crashing throb. She wasn't tired, but it hurt to think. Simply anticipating all those people coming to see her, people she couldn't remember, made her anxious.

She needed to move, she decided, to get out of this bed. If she felt more in control, she was certain she could deal with her impending visitors and all the questions they would ask.

Slowly, she slid her legs out from under the sheets and over the side of the bed. She sat, felt her blood pound in her head, then slowly subside. Satisfied with her progress, she edged her bare feet to the cool tile, waited a moment and stood.

The floor felt steady under her, solid. Not so bad, she thought, even though her legs did feel a bit shaky and her head a little fuzzy. She was certain she could manage a few steps, stretch a few muscles, then slip back under the covers.

She made it to the end of the bed and her success made her a little too smug. She turned—or at least she *thought* she was turning.

Instead, her knees buckled.

She was a split second away from meeting the floor when a strong pair of arms scooped her up.

"Whoa." Shane lifted her, held her firmly against his chest. "What are you doing out of bed?"

"I—I just wanted to stretch my legs."

And what great legs they were, Shane thought, letting his gaze sweep down the long length of slender curves to her soft-pink-painted toes. The white cotton hospital gown that covered her from neck to mid-thigh was as far from sexy as it got, but that didn't seem to matter. His blood stirred at the sight of her, and his pulse quickened.

It was the second time he'd held her in his arms. The first time had been professional; he'd had a job to do and he'd been completely focused on getting her safely out of the building. This time he felt anything but professional and his focus was not on his job, but on Emily herself.

"Is this a habit of yours, Mr. Cummings?" she asked. "Rescuing maidens in distress?"

"I was just passing by." She weighed next to nothing, he thought. Quickly he realized that was what she was wearing, as well. Her skin was soft and silky. Warm. He really should put her down, he told himself. He really should.

"Just passing by my room?" she asked.

"The hospital. The doc thought I should have my lungs looked at today."

Which was true. Dr. Tuscano had told him to have someone look at his lungs. But he could have gone to any number of clinics or over to Carney Hospital, which was much closer to the marina. Instead, he'd come back to Brookline.

"How are they?"

Damn, but she was pretty, he thought. Not like a supermodel. Just pretty. Delicate and soft. "How are what?"

"Your lungs."

"Oh. Right. Fine."

"Shane." Her thick lashes dropped and a blush rose on her pale cheeks. "I'm all right now. You can put me down."

Reluctantly, he laid her back in bed, then stepped away. "So, how are you doing?"

"Not so bad now." On a sigh, she drew the covers up over her legs. "Though when I first woke up I was wondering if you'd thrown me out of that window last night rather than carried me. Is that for me?"

Shane glanced at the single red rosebud lying on the foot of her bed. When he'd walked into the room and seen her falling, he'd tossed it there. Now that he saw the two enormous bouquets she already had in her room, he felt more than foolish he'd brought it to her.

"There's a stand downstairs that sells them," he said with a shrug, and handed the flower to her. "The profits go to the children's ward. For toys and games."

"It's beautiful." Lifting the flower to her nose, she breathed in. "Thank you."

The deep red of the rose against her smooth, creamy skin made his throat go dry. Dammit, anyway. What the hell was he doing here? It wasn't as if this could go anywhere. He knew who the Barones were. Hell, anyone who lived in Boston had heard of them. What he made in six months was pocket money to Emily's family.

"I haven't even properly thanked you for saving my life." She smiled at him, then extended her hand. "Thank you."

"You're welcome." Like the rest of her, Emily's hands were fine-boned and graceful. Her fingers were long and slender, nails neat and short. Her skin soft and cool.

The jolt of lust that shot through him had Shane quickly releasing her hand. "I should let you rest."

"No, please stay." Looking suddenly embarrassed, she lowered her gaze. "I'm sorry. I didn't mean to sound so needy. It's just that I…that you're the only person who's familiar to me. It's a little overwhelming."

"You still can't remember anything?"

She shook her head. "Just what my parents told me. The doctor was hoping they might be able to help me by telling me about myself, that I worked as a secretary at Baronessa Gelati for my brother Derrick, that my mother and I had gone to lunch and shopping for my father's birthday only a few days ago. That I live in an apartment in Brookline not too far from the plant. I like pasta and chocolate éclairs, and my nickname is Em."

Closing her eyes, she laid her head back against her pillow. "It just made my head hurt."

"So stop thinking." He turned the chair beside her bed, then straddled it. "Just let your mind go somewhere else you'd rather be."

"Like where?"

"How 'bout a quiet cove somewhere? No, keep your eyes closed," he told her when she started to open them. "Or maybe an island in the Caribbean."

"An island would be nice." A smile touched the corners of her mouth as she shut her eyes again. "What does it look like?"

"Lots of tall palm trees. You can hear the fronds rustle in the balmy breeze and the waves lap on the shore. The water is so clear you can see a school of small yellow fish darting back and forth right off the shoreline. The sky is deep, deep blue.''

"There's a puffy white cloud overhead." Emily furrowed her brow in thought. "It's in the shape of a butterfly."

He watched her shoulders relax, the slow rise and fall of her breaths, then leaned forward and lowered his voice. "The sand is soft and warm against your back. There's no one around for miles and miles."

"You're there." Her voice was a little breathless. "You're swimming."

The thought of being alone on an island with Emily made his blood heat up. "The water feels great," he murmured. "Maybe you should come in and join me."

"I don't know if I can swim. I—I can't remember."

"I'll teach you if you—"

"Emily?"

Ripped from her island fantasy, Emily opened her eyes and watched as a young woman pushed open the door. When she hurried forward, Shane quickly stood and moved out of the way.

"Emily, thank God you're all right." The woman reached for Emily's hand. "I've been so worried since Mama called. Daniel's here, too, but I made him drop me off downstairs before he parked his car. Oh, sweetheart, you're so pale."

Her eyes were the same deep blue as the silk suit jacket and skirt she wore, Emily noted. Tall and slender, probably in her late twenties. She'd pulled back her mass of blond hair in a clip on top of her head, but several thick strands escaped in a riot of loose curls around her strikingly beautiful face.

A man entered the room then, around six foot, with brown hair and the same blue eyes as the woman's. She knew this man was her other brother's twin, but they were obviously too different in appearance to be identical. Though his clothes were casual—black slacks and a white polo shirt—he had an air of old money about him.

"Hey, Em." His tone was easy, but there was concern in his steady gaze. "How's the head?"

It was starting to throb again. "It's all right."

"Do you know who I am?" he asked carefully.

"You're my brother. Daniel." Emily studied the handsome man's face, recognized the similarities between him and her father, then looked at the woman who was sitting on the side of her bed. With her hair and eyes, she looked more like their mother. "And you're Claudia. My sister."

Smiling brightly, Claudia gave Emily a gentle hug, then shot her brother a look. "I told you she'd know who we are."

"Of course she knows who we are. Mom told her we were coming. The question is—" Daniel lifted a brow "—does she *remember* us?"

"Well, of course she does, silly. How can she not remember her own brother and—" Claudia went still, then narrowed her eyes. "Omigod, you *don't* remember who we are, do you?"

Desperately Emily wanted to be back on that beach with Shane. Away from all the questions and the stares. "I—I'm sorry. I'm sure it's just temporary."

"Of course it's temporary." Claudia squeezed Emily's hand. "We're just so relieved you're all right, that the firemen were able to get you out in time."

"Shane found me." Emily glanced over to where he'd been standing only a few moments ago.

He wasn't there.

"Who?" Claudia looked over her shoulder.

"Shane. The fireman who carried me out of the building."

"Where is he?" Daniel asked. "I'd like to thank him for saving my baby sister."

Clutching the red rose he'd given her, Emily stared at the open doorway. "He's gone."

Three

A glass of mint iced tea in her hand and a paperback book in her lap, Emily lay on the chaise longue beside her parents' swimming pool. The May day was warm, the air scented with roses and a vine of blooming jasmine that spilled over a wrought-iron trellis leading to her mother's newly planted vegetable garden. Pots filled with white phlox and purple petunias surrounded the brick patio, while water bubbled from the mouth of a leaping bronze dolphin, then trickled down into a three-tiered fountain.

Emily had been told that the fountain had been last year's birthday gift from her to her mother, that two weeks ago she'd helped plant bulbs in the garden, that only three days before her accident she'd stopped by after leaving work to drop off some pictures she'd taken at Easter.

They'd shown her photo album after photo album, videotapes of parties and family barbecues, pictures of her own apartment in Brookline. They'd made her favorite foods and played the music from *Carmen,* the last opera she'd attended with her parents.

She remembered none of it.

She'd been released from the hospital five days ago. After two days of tests and monitoring, Dr. Tuscano had concluded there was nothing physically wrong with her patient. The cut on her temple was healing well, her headaches were gone and all vital signs were normal. This morning she'd noticed that even the bruises scattered on her body were beginning to fade to pale yellow and soft blue.

How odd it had been to look in the mirror that first time and see a stranger staring back. Even though she'd prepared herself, she'd still been startled and a little frightened. She'd touched her chin-length dark brown hair, her cheeks, her lips, needed to make sure she wasn't dreaming, that all of this wasn't a dream.

Or a nightmare.

But Shane had been real. That much she knew. He hadn't returned to the hospital after that last visit, or called her, either. She'd wanted so badly to see him again. Just one more time. Her family had meant well by fussing over her, but she was still confused by what had happened, still unsure of herself and what she was going to do. When Shane had been there, she'd felt calmer, more in control.

Let your mind go somewhere else, he'd told her.

She went there now. Back to her Caribbean island. The birdsong from her mother's maple tree and the trickling water from the fountain made it easier to visualize her tropical paradise. She could feel the warm sand on her back. Hear the waves lap at the shore, see the yellow hibiscus sway in the breeze. The sun had begun to dip low on the horizon, turning the ocean into a sea of dancing stars. Shane rose up from the silvery water, his muscled shoulders and arms rippling as he dragged his hands back through his hair. He had the body of an athlete, a swimmer, lean and solid, defined.

Very well defined, she thought as he walked toward her. The tan cutoffs he wore were plastered to his hips and thighs, leaving little to her imagination. She smiled. Or should she say *a lot* to the imagination.

He stood over her, held out his arm to her. She placed her hand in his and rose up to meet him, then lifted her face as he lowered his. His mouth was gentle and tasted of salt and fresh air. When his tongue slipped between her lips, she opened to him, leaned into the warmth of his body and the heat of his kiss. His arms, wet and strong and so powerful, enclosed her, pulled her firmly against him—

"Emily." Sandra Barone's cheerful voice rang out. "I've brought you some soup and a sandwich."

Jolted out of her fantasy, Emily spilled the iced tea she held in her hand. Her heart pounded as much from being startled as from her daydreaming about Shane.

"Oh, dear." Sandra set down the tray on a small glass patio table and quickly handed her daughter a linen napkin. "I'm sorry I frightened you. I thought you heard me coming."

"It's all right." Emily set her glass on the brick

decking, then dabbed at the spilled tea on the chaise cushion. "I, ah, must have fallen asleep."

"Well, I certainly hope so." Her mother slid the table closer to the chaise. "I hear you walking the hallways and downstairs at night, plus you've barely eaten enough to keep a kitten alive. I made you egg salad today and minestrone. You used to love my minestrone."

Despite the fact she wasn't hungry, Emily tasted a spoonful of the soup and forced a smile. "It's delicious. Thank you."

"Emily." Sandra sat down on the chaise beside her daughter. "You were never one to hide your feelings very well. You may not remember me right now, but I'm still your mother. You don't have to pretend with me."

"It's been a week." Emily stared at the spoon in her hand, then looked into her mother's soft blue eyes. "I haven't remembered one thing. Not you, not Dad. Not this house. Nothing."

"It's going to get better, sweetheart," Sandra said. "Easier. Some things just take time."

"And what if it doesn't get better?" Emily asked quietly. "What if I don't ever remember?"

Sandra reached up to smooth her daughter's hair, then tucked a loose strand behind her ear. A mother's gesture, Emily thought. Caring and tender. And still, Emily thought miserably, she felt nothing for this woman beyond appreciation.

"Why don't we just take one day at a time right now?" her mother suggested. "I know we've all been smothering you these past few days. Maybe it's time we all give you some breathing room, let you work this out yourself. If your head isn't speaking to you, why don't you just listen to your heart?''

"Thank you." Emily smiled at her mother, not a forced one this time. "I would appreciate that.''

Sandra kissed Emily's cheek, sighed, then stood. "Don't think this means I'm not worried about you, or that I won't fuss over you at least a little. You might as well tell the sun not to rise or Mrs. Carmichael not to walk her Pekinese through my front flower beds. It will simply fall on deaf ears. Now, I'll leave you to eat your soup. At least be polite and make an attempt at the sandwich. If I've done nothing else, I've raised my children with manners.''

Her back straight, Sandra walked back through the patio French doors. Because she wanted to please her, Emily picked up the sandwich, then nibbled at it while she watched a sparrow splash in the fountain, then shake its feathers and fly away.

Why don't you just listen to your heart?

And what did her heart tell her?

To take action. Not to sit around. To *do* something. What?

The answer came to her easily, and quite loudly.

Cookies.

Smiling, she quickly gathered up her things, then headed for the kitchen.

"For God's sake, Shane, when the hell are you gonna learn how to cook?''

Shane turned the large firehouse oven to 425°, then tossed a box of frozen pepperoni pizza to Matt. "I am cooking,'' he said, and grabbed another box. ''And at least it's recognizable. We've still got bets going whether that meat you served last week was beef or chicken.''

''Very funny.'' Offended, Matt ripped open the box of pizza. ''You know damn well it was fish.''

''Fish? Damn, I just lost five bucks.''

''That recipe dates back to my great-grandmother,'' Matt said with a scowl. ''She prepared that dish every spring to ensure a bountiful harvest.''

''Well, see, that's where I think you've got it wrong,'' Shane said cheerfully. ''You weren't supposed to eat it, you were supposed to bury it.''

''Watch it, Cummings.'' Matt gathered up the empty pizza boxes. ''Don't you be messing with family tradition.''

He couldn't very well mess with something he didn't know anything about, Shane thought. With both his parents gone, there'd been no traditions to carry on. Unless he counted his uncle's yearly St. Patrick's Day Festival. You weren't allowed in the pub unless you wore green, ate green and drank green. It was loud and rowdy, and for a day, everyone, no matter what their heritage, was Irish.

And that was the extent of Shane's family and their traditions.

''And you better come up with something other than that packaged pudding you served yesterday,'' Matt said on his way out the kitchen door, ''or we'll all bury you.''

''It was chocolate last night,'' Shane called after Matt. ''Tonight's vanilla.''

"I'm gonna go get my shovel," Matt yelled back.

So he couldn't cook, Shane thought with a frown. Big deal. He got by just fine on frozen and fast food. But there had been a great deal of complaining lately about his meals. Maybe, just to shut everyone up, he should try to make more of an effort. At least with the dessert. He went to the pantry and looked inside. Maybe he could just disguise the pudding somehow. Make it less recognizable. He scanned the shelves. Pasta. Peas. Tuna. Corn oil. Olives. Nothing *he'd* ever eaten in a dessert.

I'm a dead man, he thought.

That was when he spotted the box of graham crackers. Bingo. Slap a few crackers on the bottom of a pan, dump the packaged pudding on top, then…what? Meringue. That was eggs, right? he asked himself. Whip up some eggs, just the whites, he thought, then dump that on top of the pudding and— Wait, didn't meringue have to be cooked? Or maybe—

"Shane?"

He turned at the sound of the quiet, feminine voice.

Emily.

His pulse tripped at the sight of her standing in the doorway holding a square white box. She wore a lavender blouse and black slacks, and looked slightly flustered.

Damn if he didn't feel a little flustered himself.

"I hope I'm not bothering you," she said awkwardly.

Dammit, why did she have to show up now, looking so pretty and so lost? He'd managed to keep away from her this past week, though he hadn't managed to keep her out of his thoughts. He'd nearly caved half a dozen times and gone to see her, then came to his senses.

He watched her worry at her lower lip and felt his heart lurch.

"You're not bothering me." Actually, he was *very* bothered, though not the same kind of bothered she was referring to.

"I just wanted to stop by and...say thank you again. For saving my life." She glanced down at the box in her hands. "I made some cookies. And some brownies, too, with chocolate frosting."

"Homemade cookies and brownies?" His mouth was already watering, though not just for the treats. "Bless you, woman. Now you've saved *my* life."

When she looked at him curiously, he grinned. "It's my night to cook. Let's just say it's not what I do best. The guys will forgive the frozen pizza if I share a few cookies with them."

Clearly, a week's rest had been good for her. Her high cheeks had a lovely bloom of rose on them, her whiskey-colored eyes sparkled with clarity. Soft, wispy bangs covered the fading bruise on her right temple and hid any sign of a scar she might have from the stitches she'd received.

An air of vulnerability still shimmered around her, Shane thought. A look of wide-eyed innocence that invoked a need to protect, to defend. A need that made him feel strangely, and ridiculously, possessive.

He moved close to her, caught the faint floral scent of her perfume. "How are you feeling?"

"Fine," she said, her tone light, her smile brave.

"Except for the little detail that, despite my family's best efforts to remind me, I still don't know who I am."

Is that really why she'd come here? he asked himself. Not so much to say thank you, but to get away from her family?

And did he care?

She was here, that was all that really mattered.

His fingers itched to touch her. But this was hardly the time, and definitely not the place. By now, everyone in the station was aware of the fact that a beautiful woman was in the kitchen with him. There'd be comments, he knew, and while normally he would just laugh it off, the idea of anyone making lewd remarks about Emily set his teeth on edge.

"Well, I...I've got to go." She hesitated, then held the box out toward him. "Thank you."

"You're welcome. Thank you." How polite they both were, Shane thought irritably, though the lust churning inside him at the moment was anything but polite. He set the box on the long kitchen table. "Stay for a while."

"No, really. I should be going."

"Emily." With a sigh, he took her shoulders in his hands and leveled his gaze with hers. "I want you to stay."

This time the smile made it to her eyes. "Okay."

Dammit, but he wanted to kiss her. He felt the need to pull her close, knew it would be a very foolish thing to do. Yet, still he did not release her.

Emily knew she should step away from Shane's touch. Knew she should say something light or casual, anything to break the sudden spell she found herself under. At the very least, she told herself, she should look away from the blue-green gaze he had locked on her.

But she couldn't move. Could barely breathe, for that matter. It felt so right to be here with him, for his hands to be on her. The anticipation that he might kiss her made her pulse begin to race.

"Emily," he said softly. "I need to—"

He paused, lowered his gaze to her mouth.

"What?" She let her head tip back, felt her lips open ever so slightly....

His hands tightened, then dropped away. "Check my pizza."

"Oh. Of course."

She was still holding her breath, she realized, and slowly released it when he turned away. She felt utterly ridiculous, and was glad his back was to her while she struggled to regain her composure. When he opened the oven, the aroma of Italian spices and melting cheese wafted out. The scents were familiar to her and she found them comforting as she wandered around the neat, spacious kitchen.

On the wall beside the refrigerator, snapshots and various announcements were pinned to a large cork bulletin board. Emily smiled at the picture of a baby girl named Martha on a birth announcement, then read the flyer beside it for an upcoming fireman's bachelor auction at the Boston Marriott on the Long Wharf.

"I'll give you a tour after we eat." Shane shifted

the pizzas around in the oven, then closed the door again. "Should be ready in about ten minutes."

"I'm not staying to eat." Just the thought of sitting around this big table with a crew of firefighters made her heart jump. "I really couldn't. I just—"

"You think you can remember how to make a salad?"

"I— Of course I do."

"Then you're staying. Lettuce and tomatoes are in the fridge drawer, and whatever else you can find. Personally, I could do without it, but some of the guys are convinced it's necessary." He opened a cupboard and pulled out an armload of plates. "Unless you'd rather set the table."

"The salad is fine." After a week of sitting around being waited on, Emily felt almost giddy with something to make herself feel useful.

She found everything she needed, including a large bowl, and began to chop tomatoes, green peppers and mushrooms. She and Shane worked in amiable silence for a few minutes, and though she thought it odd that none of the other men had come into the kitchen, she suspected they were keeping their distance until dinnertime because of her.

She was grateful to all these men. Every one of them risked his life every time he went out on a call. In spite of the fact she'd lost her memory, she still knew that she was one of the lucky ones, that without them she wouldn't be standing here at all.

She'd wanted to personally thank all the firemen for fighting the fire, and though the cookies had been an inspiration, she knew she'd especially wanted to see Shane. She'd even called the station before she came down to make sure he was working.

"Has the cause of the fire been determined yet?" she asked while she sliced a tomato.

"Nothing definite yet," he said. "It's still under investigation."

She glanced over at him, watched him move back and forth to the cupboards and drawers as he set the table. The instant butterflies in her stomach made her feel like an infatuated teenager. She knew that she shouldn't be here, but after a week in her parents' house, she'd needed desperately to get out, if only for a little while.

"One of the nurses mentioned you own a boat." She reached for a bell pepper. The nurses had mentioned other things about Shane, as well. That he was single and had never been married, that he'd dated a few of the nurses from the hospital, and that any woman who wanted to become Mrs. Shane Cummings had better take a number and wait in line.

And according to the nurses, it looked as if it would be a long wait.

"I've got a sloop at Boston Harbor Marina." He moved beside her and reached for a pitcher in an overhead cupboard. "Ever been on a sailboat?"

"I don't know."

He set the pitcher on the counter, then took her chin in his hand and tilted her face upward. "Maybe that's the fun of losing your memory," he said with a smile. "Everything's a new experience."

"I hadn't quite looked at it that way." She smiled back. "But it's certainly true."

"You'll remember, Emily," he said softly.

"What if I don't?"

"Then you don't." He traced her jaw with his thumb. "You just move forward, one day at a time, and build new memories. My shift ends tomorrow. I'll take you sailing."

"You don't have to do that."

"Of course I don't have to. I want to." He lifted a brow. "Is there someone who'd rather I didn't?"

She furrowed her brow in confusion. "I don't understand."

"If I'm going to make a boyfriend jealous, I'd at least like to know ahead of time."

"Oh." Emily had learned from her sister that she'd dated someone named Jeffrey for a few months, but they'd broken up several months before the fire. "No. There's no one."

"Then I'll pick you up in the early afternoon."

"I'd like that." Heavens. She wasn't even trying to be coy. She was practically throwing herself at Shane. And she didn't care.

Had she been this brazen before? she wondered. It was difficult to imagine, but certainly anything was possible.

As his hand lingered on her chin, the awareness shimmered between them again, just as it had only a few minutes ago. It frightened her how much she wanted this man to hold her, to kiss her. To tell her everything would be all right.

The oven buzzer sounded, but Shane ignored it.

"There is one thing I'll bet you've never done before," he murmured.

"What's that?"

"Had dinner surrounded by twelve burly firemen."

She laughed softly. "I'll bet you're right."

"Prepare yourself, Miss Barone." He dropped his hand away. "You are about to have what will most definitely be a memorable experience."

Four

The two-story brick house sat back from a shady, maple-lined street. The lawn was manicured, the flower beds as colorful as they were meticulous. The neighborhood of stately homes was dignified and definitely upscale.

When he was seventeen, Shane had dated a girl who lived in this neighborhood. Megan Worthington. He'd been working at the South Shore Yacht Club, scrubbing boat decks and running errands for the members, plus waiting tables in the private restaurant and helping out in the kitchen. Megan had been blond and bubbly and two years older than he. Shane had thought he'd loved Megan, and that she loved him, until her parents offered her a brand-new Porsche if she dissolved the relationship. One week later, while

Megan was enjoying her new car, Shane was out a girlfriend *and* a job.

Such are the lessons of life, he thought with a shrug.

Shaking his head at the memory, Shane pulled his Mustang convertible into the driveway of Sandra and Paul Barone's house and parked. He still wasn't sure what he was doing here. He'd told himself a dozen times it would serve no purpose for Emily or himself to see each other again, then suddenly he'd asked her to go sailing with him.

She'd just looked as if she could use some fresh air and sunshine, he thought. A few hours out on the ocean, away from everything. Who knows, he thought as he climbed out of his car. Maybe if she relaxed, her memory would come back. When it did, of course, she'd go back to her own world, he was certain of that. But what the hell. The truth was he wanted to be with her.

He wouldn't get involved with Emily. That would be stupid. But he could enjoy her company for an afternoon, couldn't he? And she seemed to want to be with him, too, although he suspected more than anything else she was just feeling grateful toward him.

Whatever it was she felt toward him, or he felt toward her, it didn't really matter. He'd take her sailing, and that would be that.

Shane rang the doorbell of the Barone residence, noticed a lace curtain flutter from a front room window, then a moment later the door opened.

The woman smiling at him wore a blue silk blouse

and black tailored pants. Her eyes were the same color as her blouse, and her wavy blond hair was tucked neatly back from her elegant face with a tortoiseshell headband.

"Mr. Cummings." The woman held out her hand. "Sandra Barone. I can't tell you what a pleasure it is to finally meet you. Please, come in."

The house inside was as refined as its mistress, Shane thought as he took in the sweeping staircase, glossy wood floors, high ceilings, carved moldings and leaded glass windows. Through a pair of French doors leading to a patio, Shane noticed three women sitting at a table.

"I haven't yet properly thanked you for saving my daughter's life," Sandra said. "There are no words to express my gratitude."

Shane shifted uncomfortably. "It's not necessary. I was doing my job."

"I was told you carried her out only moments before an explosion. If you hadn't found her, she would have—" Her voice broke and moisture filled her eyes.

"I did find her, Mrs. Barone," Shane said quietly. "And she's fine. In time, I'm sure her memory will come back, too."

Sandra nodded, then drew in a slow breath and smiled. "Could I persuade you to join my bridge club for tea and sandwiches before you and Emily run off? They'd love to hear all about Emily's rescue firsthand."

Tea and sandwiches with the bridge club? He glanced at the small china cups and plates of finger sandwiches on the table. He'd rather jump off a fifty-foot pier into shark-infested waters. "Ah, thank you, but we should really—"

"Shane."

He turned as Emily appeared at the top of the stairway. She wore white capris and a soft green T-shirt, and carried a canvas bag over her shoulder.

Just the sight of her made his throat go dry. He felt suddenly anxious, like a teenager picking up his first date.

"Hi." She kept her gaze on his as she moved down the stairs. "I'm sorry if I kept you waiting."

"I just got here."

Emily stepped toward her mother and kissed her cheek. "I'll call you later."

"All right." But there was worry in Sandra's eyes as she glanced at her daughter. "Have fun, dear. If you need me, you can call my cell phone, or you can reach your father at the office, or—"

"I'm *fine,*" Emily said firmly. "Stop worrying."

"It's my job," Sandra said with a sigh, then turned at the sound of her name being called from outside. "Well, all right, then. I'll see you later."

Sandra hurried off and Emily turned toward Shane. "I forgot my jacket. I'll be right back."

He stared after her as she walked back up the stairs, couldn't help but notice the sway of her hips and the snug fit of her capris across her backside. Her legs were long and curved and he wondered what they'd feel like wrapped around his waist while he—

"Cummings."

Shane clenched his jaw, then turned slowly at the sound of the deep voice.

Derrick Barone.

Emily's brother stood in the doorway leading to a living area. His slacks were neatly pressed, his button-down white cotton shirt starched. Keeping his gaze on Shane, Derrick took a sip from the glass of amber liquid in his hand.

"I heard you're taking Emily sailing."

"That's right."

"My sister's not well." Disapproval narrowed Derrick's eyes as he moved into the foyer. "She should be resting."

"Is that your medical opinion," Shane asked evenly, "or your personal opinion?"

Derrick pressed his lips together. "I have a right to an opinion, Cummings. Which is more than I can say for you. My only motive is for Emily to get well. What's yours?"

Though Shane would like nothing better than to stuff Derrick's glass down his Ivy League throat, he wouldn't. Not here, at least. He replied, "Your sister's a beautiful woman and I like being with her."

"Or maybe you see a confused, vulnerable woman who's misplaced her gratitude." The ice in Derrick's glass clinked as he tossed back a drink. "Or maybe you like the fact that her trust fund generates more income in one month than you make in a year."

Maybe I was wrong, Shane thought. Maybe he would have to stuff that glass down Derrick's throat, after all. Of course, that would mean he wouldn't get to take Emily sailing, and most likely he'd never see her again, but he didn't expect he'd see her after today, anyway.

So what the hell.

Fear lit Derrick's eyes when Shane started toward him.

"I'm ready," Emily said brightly as she came back down the stairs. Shane stopped but kept his gaze on Derrick, who had already taken a step back. Emily moved between the two men, glanced at Shane, then at her brother. "Is everything all right?"

"Everything's fine," Shane said dryly. "Your brother and I were just getting to know each other a little better. Isn't that right, Derrick?"

Derrick forced a smile and lifted his glass. "That's right, sis."

Shane dragged his attention back to Emily, wondering how in the hell she could be related to such a jerk. "Shall we go?"

Emily cast a nervous glance between her brother and Shane, then nodded.

"Don't wait up," Shane said to Derrick as he touched the small of Emily's back and guided her to the front door. "We might be late."

Behind him, Shane could all but hear Derrick gnashing his teeth.

Next time the bastard started something, Shane thought, not even Emily would be able to save him.

"It seems that I'm indebted to you once again," Emily told Shane as he held open the door of his shiny black Mustang convertible. "My mother wanted me to join her bridge club."

Shane closed the door, then came around and slid

behind the wheel. He stared through his windshield, his hands tightly on the wheel, his jaw clenched.

Emily bit her lower lip. What had she said? "Shane, I—I know you're busy, and you've already been so generous with your time for me. I'll understand if you'd rather not—"

"Let's get something straight." He turned to look at her. "You're not indebted to me for anything. I was doing my job when I pulled you out of that building. It could have been any woman, or any man. It's what I get paid to do."

She didn't understand why he was so angry. And she had the feeling that he wasn't just upset with her, but with himself, too.

"I'm sorry," she said quietly. "I shouldn't have come to the station. I realize how pathetic I must appear, and I've put you in a difficult—"

"Emily, for God's sake." He took hold of her shoulders and forced her to look at him. "This isn't a pity date. I'm here with you because I want to be. You got that?"

She nodded. Was this actually a *date?* she wondered. The idea of it made her stomach flutter. She felt his hands settle gently on her arms, then slide away.

He started the car and turned up his radio—to discourage any conversation, she assumed. She knew what he'd told her was true, that he'd simply been doing his job when he'd carried her out of the building, that it wouldn't have mattered who she was.

Still, whether he wanted her gratitude or not, he had it. How could she not value the fact he'd saved her life? But her feelings went beyond gratitude, of that she was certain. From the moment she'd opened her eyes—at the fire and the hospital—and her gaze had met his, she'd felt a connection with him. She couldn't explain it; she could only feel it.

Shane was the only person with whom she felt completely safe.

If she told him that, she knew he'd run for the hills. She'd learned enough about Shane Cummings from the nurses at the hospital to know he wasn't looking for any kind of relationship. Prettier, smarter women than she had certainly tried to hook the sexy fireman and failed. She'd simply be happy with the moment, she decided. Riding in his car with the top down while Nirvana and Red Hot Chili Peppers blasted from his radio.

They wound through city streets, jumped on the freeway, then exited at the Boston Harbor Marina sign. Emily took it all in: the busy parking lot, the crowds strolling along the dock, the scent of damp, salty air and the screech of seagulls floating overhead.

It felt new, yet at the same time, familiar.

They walked past families snapping photographs and a tour group buying hot dogs.

"You hungry?" Shane asked her when she paused to watch a teenage girl squeezing ketchup on a paper tray of French fries.

"Thank you, no. It's just...I'm having a sense of déjà vu, I think. I feel as if I've been here before."

"Maybe you have," he said. "With your family, or maybe a boyfriend."

"My sister told me I dated a man named Jeffrey

for a few months,'' Emily said, still watching the teenager. ''But we broke up six months ago. I don't remember anything about him, or why we broke up.''

''Bad for Jeffrey.'' Shane took her hand, then brought her fingers to his lips. ''Good for me.''

The press of his lips on her knuckles sent a thrill through Emily. She knew it was silly to let a simple flirtation mean so much, but she couldn't help herself. She felt foolish and pathetic and absolutely wonderful.

With his hand still holding hers, he tugged her along the dock. Several boat owners waved or called out greetings to Shane as they passed. He waved back but didn't stop to chat or introduce her. He bought sandwiches and chips from a vendor, then moved on again. They were nearly at the end of the dock when he stopped. ''Here we are.''

They stood in front of a lovely, single-mast sailboat, more than thirty feet, Emily could tell, with a glossy teak deck and railings.

Free Spirit.

A wonderful name, Emily thought.

Shane stepped over the railing and offered her his hand, then led her down the companionway steps to the deck below. When they reached the bottom of the stairs, she gasped. ''You have everything here. A sink and a stove. Even a fridge!''

''It's called the galley.'' He opened a narrow door to the left of the steps. ''This is the water closet, more commonly known as the head.''

Emily glanced through the door. There was a small sink and a handheld shower. She noticed the bottle of shampoo on a shelf, a half-empty tube of toothpaste sitting beside a comb and razor, and a white bath towel slung over a shower bar.

That was when it hit her.

"You live here?" Amazed, she turned back to face him. "On your boat?"

"It keeps life simple," he said with a shrug. "No grass to mow or bushes to trim."

No wife, no kids. No homey touches or frills. He might as well have named the ship, *The Bachelor*. She glanced around the small cabin, then asked, "Where's your bed?"

She would have called the question back if she hadn't already blurted it out. Had she always been so forward with men? she wondered. Or was it just Shane who made her feel so casual and spontaneous?

"Actually," he said with a grin, "it's called a berth."

He took her hand again and led her to the bow of the boat. A deep green comforter neatly covered the king-size bed. The walls were paneled with dark wood and a beige throw rug lay on the floor beside the bed. She noticed a book on a built-in nightstand and a pair of well-worn running shoes tossed carelessly at the foot of the mattress.

Like he'd told her, he kept his life simple. He didn't even have any pictures on the walls.

And yet at the same time it was cozy, she thought. Comfortable. She wondered what it would feel like to stretch out on that big bed of his, to close her eyes and let the gentle rocking of the boat lull her to sleep.

And then he stepped closer and she wasn't thinking about sleep at all.

Energy radiated from his body. And heat. Her heart started to pound fiercely when he lifted a hand to her face and lightly traced her cheekbone with the tip of his finger.

"You have the softest skin," he murmured.

"Thank you." Shivering at his touch, she tilted her head back and met his gaze. His fingertip trailed down her jaw to her chin, and she slowly leaned into him, waiting....

"Sunscreen." He dropped his hand away.

She blinked. "What?"

"Did you bring sunscreen?" He glanced down at the bag she'd slung over her shoulder. "I think I have some if you didn't."

"Oh. Right." She gathered her wits and drew in a breath. "Yes. I brought a tube."

"Good. Make sure you put lots on. How 'bout a hat?"

How was it she'd so quickly gone from feeling like a woman to a child? "I forgot a hat."

He moved to a small closet and took out a Red Sox baseball cap, adjusted the size, then pulled it snugly over her head.

With a grin, he stepped back. "Ready?"

Though her heart was still pounding and her skin was still tingling, she grinned back. "Aye-aye, Captain."

They motored out of the marina, a slow *putt-putt-putt*, until they passed the breakwater, then Shane turned off the motor. Emily, seated at the helm, watched while Shane climbed up on deck and hoisted the mainsail.

The afternoon sun glistened silver off the gentle ocean swells. The fresh air invigorated Emily, heightening her senses. The sky seemed bluer, the water clearer. She drew the briny scent of the sea into her lungs, closed her eyes and felt the soft breeze flutter across her face.

"Ready?" Shane asked when he came back down from the deck.

Opening her eyes, she glanced over her shoulder at him. "Ready?"

"Here." He stepped close behind her, took hold of her hands and lifted them to the helm. "Hold tight."

With his hands covering her own, Shane turned the wheel.

Emily's heart jumped when the boat caught a gust and lurched.

"That's called a heel over," he said with a chuckle. "Now we have some fun."

Free Spirit picked up the wind and moved, tipping to one side as it glided smoothly over the ocean. Emily laughed at the incredible sense of exhilaration pumping wildly through her veins. A sense of complete and utter freedom.

She leaned back into the solid strength of Shane's body and let the cool mist of the ocean air slide over her face. Here, she didn't have to think about who she was or what her life was like before. She could simply *be*. And with Shane, it felt so right.

As if she belonged.

"We'll have lunch there," he said, pointing to a

small island ahead. Emily had lost track of time, wasn't certain if minutes or hours had passed since they'd left the harbor. Nor did she really care.

Fascinated, she watched as Shane expertly and carefully maneuvered into a small, private cove, then lowered the mainsail and anchored the boat at shore. He went belowdecks for a few moments, then came back up with a blanket, the sandwiches he'd bought at the dock and two bottles of water.

She took off her canvas shoes and they waded through the cool, shallow water to a beach where he spread out the blanket. They were surrounded by high, jagged rocks and warm, clean sand. A light breeze carried the scent of the ocean.

They were alone.

"Shane, this is so beautiful," she said after they settled on the blanket. "How did you ever find this place?"

"Dumb luck. It's too small to be on any map. I was actually looking for another island I'd heard rumors about when I stumbled on this one. There's rarely anyone here."

When he tugged his T-shirt up over his head and pulled it off, Emily's breath caught. His arms were muscled, his chest broad, with a sprinkling of dark hair that narrowed to his waist, then disappeared at the snap of his beige denim shorts. His legs were long and powerful, his skin tanned golden.

She wanted to touch him, she realized. Wanted him to touch her.

Startled by her thought, and because she didn't want to stare, she glanced away.

"How long have you been with the fire department?" Instead of Shane's muscled body, Emily kept her gaze on the ocean waves lapping at the shore.

"Five years." Stretching out his long legs, he lay back on the blanket and folded his hands underneath his head.

"Why did you choose the fire department?"

"It chose me, really. My dad was a fireman, so it's in my blood."

"*Was* a fireman?"

"He was killed in a warehouse fire ten years ago. The roof caved in after an explosion."

"I'm so sorry." It frightened her how close history had nearly come to repeating itself for Shane. He'd barely made it out of the building he'd rescued her from a little more than a week ago. "It must be hard for your mother, losing her husband and now worrying about her son."

"I suppose it would be, if she were alive," he said quietly. "She lost a battle with cancer a few years ago. I think she just didn't have it in her to fight after my dad died."

"Oh, Shane." Lying back on the blanket beside him, she had no idea what to say, but the need to comfort overwhelmed her. When she touched his shoulder, he tensed, then slowly relaxed when she lightly stroked his skin. "Do you have other family?"

"No sisters or brothers. Just my mother's brother, Darcy."

Realizing that she was still touching Shane, and how presumptuous it must seem to him, Emily started to pull her hand away, but he quickly reached up and snagged it back.

"When I was a kid," he said, absently toying with her fingers, "my mom would have him over every Sunday night. I have a lot of great memories of those dinners and holidays."

Would she ever have the memories of her own childhood back? Emily wondered. Would she ever remember where she'd come from, all the things she'd done? Family dinners, the names of teachers, classmates. The first boy she'd ever kissed...

She lifted her gaze to Shane, saw him watching her intently. He'd gone from toying with her fingers to stroking her hand. She knew she should pull away, but couldn't.

Fantasy had become reality for her. Lying on a deserted beach with Shane, the warm sand underneath, the sun overhead.

But the fantasy wasn't complete, she thought. Close, but not quite.

"Shane, would you—" Suddenly shy, she dropped her gaze. "Would you please kiss me?"

Five

Would he kiss her?

Kissing her was all he'd thought about for the past week. Well, he'd thought about other things he'd like to do to her, too, but every time he had, he'd forced his mind in another direction, any direction that would keep him from wondering what Emily would taste like, what her body would feel like underneath his own.

He'd somehow managed to resist her belowdecks, before they'd taken the boat out, but now, as he watched her cheeks bloom pink with embarrassment, as she dropped her gaze from his and caught her lower lip between her teeth, he knew he could resist her no longer.

She tried to pull her hand from his, but he held her still.

"I—I'm sorry, Shane." She turned her head away. "That was extremely forward of me. I wasn't thinking and I—"

"Good." He rose on an elbow, slowly slid his fingers up her arm, her shoulder, her neck, then cupped the base of her head in his hand. "Don't think."

He lowered his head to hers, watched her eyes widen, then drift close as his lips touched hers. He took his time, nibbled lightly at the corner of her mouth, then traced the soft curve of her lips. When she sighed, he slipped inside.

Sweet, he thought. Incredibly, unbelievably sweet.

Damn. He'd suspected that kissing Emily might be dangerous. But what he hadn't known was just how devastating her effect on him would be. He thought he'd at least be able to control his need for her. What harm was there in a kiss?

What an idiot he was.

When she made a small sound from deep in her throat, a soft moan, he lost it altogether.

He leaned over her, stretching his body over hers as he deepened the kiss. Her arms came around his shoulders, tentatively at first, then tighter. He felt the sun on his back and the light brush of her fingertips on his neck. She shuddered underneath him and he knew he could take her right here, that she wanted him as badly as he wanted her.

The thought was like a cold wave washing over him. He couldn't do this. Emily was confused, she didn't know who she was, for God's sake. That was the only reason she'd turned to him. He'd be taking advantage of her, of the situation.

Dammit. He'd vowed to take her away from her troubles today, and all he'd done was create more.

Slowly, he eased away from her, then sat up. Her eyes, still glazed over from his kiss, fluttered open. He stared out at the white-capped ocean, waited a moment for all the blood that had gone south to even out again.

"Are you wearing a swimsuit?" he asked when he finally managed to find his voice.

She sat beside him, lifted a trembling hand to smooth back the strands of hair rippling across her face. "Yes."

"Good." He stood, glanced down at her. "You've got two minutes to get your clothes off and be out in the water, or I'm coming back to get you."

He walked toward the shoreline and dove into the water, wishing to God it was colder. He groaned as he looked back and watched Emily step tentatively out of her capris, then slowly peel off her T-shirt. She wore a bright pink one-piece suit cut high on the sides, which made her already long legs look endless. Because he was only human, he scanned upward from her legs to her narrow waist, then higher still to her breasts, breasts that would fit a man's hands perfectly.

His hands, he thought.

He reminded himself he needed to keep his hands *off*, not *on* her, then dove under the water and shook his head before he broke for the surface again.

But not even the cool water and the damp, salty air could erase the taste of her in his mouth or the feel of her body against his. He'd made a mistake, he knew, and he'd pay for it.

He glanced her way, watched her step carefully into the water, then hug her arms in front of her, completely unaware that her breasts nearly spilled out from the top of her bathing suit.

With a groan, he ducked back under the water and began counting to ten.

He might be able to keep her out of his life, he thought, but he wasn't so sure he'd be able to keep her out of his mind.

"Em, are you sure you don't want me to come up with you? Just for a few minutes? I could fix dinner for you. I won't even stay if you don't want me to. Maybe show you around?"

"Claudia, I'm fine." Emily sat in the front seat of her sister's sedan and stared at the Brookline brownstone apartment house they'd parked in front of. The paint on the white shuttered windows was fresh and glossy, the small front flower garden well kept. A wrought-iron gate opened to a brick walkway, which led to the front entrance. Historic lampposts and tall maples lined the street.

A beautiful neighborhood, Emily thought.

And despite the fact that she'd lived here for the past three years, it wasn't remotely familiar.

"I'm coming up," Claudia said when Emily continued to stare at the apartment building. "This is your first time back. You might remember something and I could—"

"No." Emily shook her head. "I have to do this by myself. It's difficult to explain, but I need to be alone for a little while."

It had taken Emily four days to convince her
mother and father that she needed to do this. She understood it was their love for her that made her family
so protective, but in spite of all their concern and care,
they were still like strangers to her. The strain of pretending to be all right on the outside, when on the
inside she was still frightened and confused, had become too much.

"How 'bout I just walk with you up to your door?"
Claudia said.

"No."

"Carry your suitcase?"

"Absolutely not."

"I could—"

"*Claudia.*"

"All right." Claudia sighed. "Jeez. You never
used to be this stubborn. This is going to take some
getting used to."

"That goes for two of us." Smiling, Emily reached
across and gave her sister a hug. "I'll be fine. Stop
worrying."

"You promised to call Mom in an hour."

"I will."

"You've got Mom and me on your speed dial.
Daniel and Dad drove your car over last night and
it's parked in the back lot." Claudia dug in her purse
and pulled out a set of keys. "It's a blue Camry. Your
keys were lost in the fire, along with everything else
in your purse, but you've got credit cards and cash
and more checks in the top drawer of your desk. Mom
called the DMV and she's also ordered groceries to
be delivered in about an hour. If you need anything,

or if you remember something, or if you just need to—''

''Stop.'' Palm out, Emily held up her hand. ''I'm getting out now, Claudia. Goodbye.''

Before Claudia could start again, Emily stepped out of the car, then grabbed her suitcase from the back seat and headed for the front door of the apartment building.

Emily's mother had told her that the building had been split into six apartments, that hers was on the second floor, number four. She stood in the small lobby for a long moment, breathed in the scent of lemon wax and baking bread. The sound of someone practicing the cello drifted from the downstairs apartment in the rear. The place felt comfortable and homey, but it still didn't feel familiar.

As she looked up to the second floor, her knees turned to mush and her heart started to pound. She suddenly wished someone was with her. Someone she felt she could lean on. Not Claudia or her mother or father.

Shane.

She'd thought of him all week, had smiled every time she recalled their sailing excursion. Every time she thought about the way he'd kissed her, the way he'd held her close in his arms, she'd felt flushed and tingly. She was certain she'd been kissed before, for heaven's sake. But those memories were all gone now. For her, Shane's kiss had been a first kiss. Exciting and wonderful and thrilling.

She'd thrown herself at him, she knew. Had actually *asked* him to kiss her. And then when he had, she'd wanted more.

He obviously hadn't.

They'd swum and eaten lunch and sailed back to the marina, then he'd taken her home. He'd politely walked her to her front door, told her to take care, then he'd left. He hadn't kissed her good-night, hadn't told her he'd call.

She didn't blame him. Though she didn't think she was unattractive, she certainly wasn't a femme fatale, either. Shane obviously preferred a different type of woman from herself. Like, maybe one who could re-member her own name?

A phone rang from one of the downstairs apart-ments and pulled her wandering mind back to the task at hand. Emily took a deep breath, then moved up the carpeted staircase. She found her apartment in the front of the building and slid the key her mother had given her this morning into the lock. The door swung open.

She stepped inside.

And felt something.

She couldn't say exactly *what* she felt, but it was *something*. As if she had been here before. The floors were polished oak, the walls off-white. The sofa in her living area was tan-and-white stripes, with green-and-burgundy floral and plaid pillows. Setting her suitcase down, she moved into the room and ran her fingers over the soft fabric of a plaid, forest-green easy chair, then glanced at the books on her coffee table: *Famous Boston Gardens, New England Amer-icana, The History of Clocks and Watches.*

She moved to the bookshelves on the wall behind her. They were filled with mysteries and thrillers, classics, romances and contemporary women's fiction, as well as nonfiction. Obviously, she liked to read.

She spent the next hour exploring. Her kitchen was bright and cheerful, with lots of cookbooks that appeared well used. Her bathroom was large, with a restored ball-and-claw bathtub beside an antique dresser that had been converted to a lavatory. She had a small guest room with a double bed and a writing desk. Her own bedroom had striped pink wallpaper and a queen-size four-poster bed with a floral comforter.

She opened her closet and the scent of lavender potpourri drifted out. Her taste was clearly conservative. Tailored suits and pants, lots of beige and navy and off-white. She was examining a tan linen suit when she heard the doorbell.

The groceries her mother had ordered.

But it wasn't a delivery person, Emily realized as she opened the door. The woman standing there wasn't holding a bag of food, but a bouquet of flowers. She was beautiful, with long, dark brown hair and big brown eyes. The pantsuit she wore was deep blue, with a tie at the side of her narrow-waisted jacket.

"Emily." The woman's smile dipped when there was no sign of recognition on Emily's face. "It's me. Maria. Your cousin."

"Maria." Emily remembered the pictures her mother had shown her of all eight of her cousins. Close in age to Emily, Maria was her Uncle Carlo and Aunt Moira's youngest. "Yes, of course. I'm sorry, please come in."

"So it's really true, then?" Maria handed the bouquet to Emily. "You really don't remember who you are?"

Emily forced a smile. "I'm afraid so."

Maria stared at Emily for a long moment, then took her hand and pulled her into the kitchen and pointed to a chair. "Sit."

Bewildered, Emily sat, then watched as Maria pulled a vase out from under the sink and filled it with water. After she arranged the flowers, she went to another cupboard, brought out a bottle of Chianti, a corkscrew from a drawer, then two glasses.

"You've been here before," Emily said when Maria uncorked the bottle.

"Many times." Maria filled the wineglasses, then handed one to Emily. *"Salute."*

They touched glasses and sipped. The rich taste exploded in Emily's mouth. "So I do like wine."

Laughing, Maria sat at the table. "Of course you like wine. You're Italian. It's a law."

"My mother never offered me any these past several days, so I assumed I didn't drink."

"Well, you're not exactly a lush," Maria said with a smile. "But we've shared a bottle on occasion. Girls night out, parties, family dinners."

Emily took another sip of the wine, felt the warmth quickly spreading through her. Other than when she'd been with Shane, sitting at this kitchen table with Maria was the most relaxed she'd felt with another person in days. It wasn't as if she was remembering anything; she just felt…comfortable.

"Maria—" Emily looked at her cousin "—I know I'll be meeting everyone at the reunion next month, but maybe you can tell me something now about our family."

"We could be here for days," Maria said with a grin, "but you were especially close to Alex. He's a pilot with the Navy and the Blue Angels. Maybe when you see him, something will click for you."

"I certainly hope so," Emily said with a sigh. "My mother has shown me pictures, told me a few stories, but I feel as if she's keeping some things from me."

"Ah." Swirling the wine in her glass, Maria sat back. "The skeletons in the closet."

Emily nodded. "I overheard my mother and father talking about some problems with the family business, but when I asked them about it, they told me not to worry, that everything is fine. I know it's because they're concerned about me and trying to protect me, but I'd appreciate if you'd tell me the truth."

"You want the most recent scandal, or the old stuff?"

"Let's start with the recent," Emily said. "Then work our way back."

"Well, for starters, someone spiked the new gelato flavor we brought out last February with hot peppers. You can imagine the chaos that created."

"Hot pepper gelato?" Emily shuddered at the thought. "Who would do such a thing?"

"That's the burning question." Maria sat back with a sigh. "A rival company, a disgruntled employee, a crazy. Lord knows there are plenty of those around. Then there are the accusations of links to the Mafia, which are absurd, but people eat up those kinds of headlines like candy.''

Emily took another sip of wine. It appeared that the Barone family *did* have a lot to deal with.

''Let's see...'' Maria tapped a finger to her chin. ''Oh, yeah. There's the tabloid pictures of my sister Gina half-naked with Flint Kingman, Baronessa's PR consultant. My father is still fuming over that, even though they're married now.''

Emily lifted a brow at that little piece of information. She was looking forward to meeting all her cousins, though, with eight of them, maybe not all at once.

''And now the fire,'' Emily said carefully.

Maria paused, then reached across the table to touch Emily's arm. ''Em, the fire was an accident. There's been no proof of arson.''

''Shane told me it's still under investigation.''

''Shane?''

''The fireman who saved me.''

''Oh, yes.'' Smiling, Maria put her elbows on the table and leaned forward. ''There *have* been rumors.''

Emily looked up sharply. ''Rumors? What kind of rumors?''

''The good kind.'' Maria ran her index finger over the rim of her glass. ''That he's one sexy hunk and when he looks at you, there's enough heat to start a major blaze.''

Emily gasped. ''Where did you hear such a thing?''

''The Barone family has spies everywhere,'' Maria said quietly. She glanced away for a moment, lost in her own thoughts, then turned back to Emily and smiled again. "Evelyn Van Der Weilen is in your mother's bridge club. She was at your house last Sunday when your fireman came in to take you sailing. Evelyn's daughter Lucy is friends with Gina, my sister, your cousin."

It made Emily's head spin. All the names. Whose belonged to whom? It was like living in a small town, only here, everyone knew more about her than she did herself. "I'm sorry to disappoint Evelyn and Lucy, but Shane and I are just friends. I think he feels a responsibility toward me, but that's it."

"And what do you feel toward him?" Maria asked.

"I—" Emily hesitated, not sure what she should say. She hadn't told anyone her feelings for Shane. Especially since he didn't return them. "I guess I like him."

Maria winced. "You *like* him?"

"I like him." She glanced down. "A lot."

There. She'd said it.

"Now we're getting somewhere. Come on, Em. Give me something here. Has he kissed you? Oh, so he *has*," Maria said when Emily's cheeks flushed red. "And how was it?"

"It was…it was *amazing*." There it was again, that same tingle she got every time she thought about Shane's kiss. She shook the feeling off and closed her eyes. "It doesn't matter. He hasn't called, didn't even tell me he would. I don't expect I'll ever see him again. Unless…"

No. She couldn't do that.

"Unless what?" Maria asked.

She *couldn't* do that, Emily told herself. She'd only be embarrassing herself more if she did.

She chewed on her bottom lip. But which was worse? Making a fool of herself, or always wondering what could have been? She already had enough in her life to wonder about—her entire past, for starters. She didn't want to add any what-ifs to that daunting list. From what everyone had told her, and the way everyone treated her, Emily thought, she'd never been much of a take-charge person.

She had no one to blame for that but herself. Maybe she needed to start her new life by letting go of her fears. By being confident. Making decisions.

And if she wanted to start a new life, she thought she needed a new look, as well.

Emily took another sip of wine, then sat straight. "Maria, do you think you could spare some time tomorrow? I have a project I could use your assistance with."

"Of course. I'll find someone to cover for me at work." Maria cocked her head and lifted a brow. "You want to tell me?"

"Tomorrow," Emily said firmly. "Tonight I'd like to hear more about our family's deep, dark secrets."

"Why don't we order a pizza? You like mushroom and bell pepper, by the way. At least, you used to." Maria was already reaching for the kitchen wall phone. "I'm a pepperoni gal, myself."

Maria ordered the pizza, then hooked an arm through Emily's and pulled her toward the living room. "We need to get comfortable, cousin. This is going to take a while."

Six

He hated tuxedos.

They were stiff, too tight in the collar, and he could never get the bow tie right. He'd rather jump out of a burning second-story window, in full gear, with no net, than put one of these monkey suits on.

If it wasn't for charity, Shane thought, he'd be ten miles out of the marina at this very moment. On his way to Wilson Island, or maybe taking a run up to Cape Ann. Or maybe he would have headed out to open sea. He rarely had a plan when he went out, preferring instead to let the wind and his gut decide.

Stretching his neck, he glanced around the crowded ballroom of the Boston Marriott Long Wharf. A ten-piece band played a mix of fifties and sixties music, and the dance floor was crowded with wealthy businessmen and women—women outnumbering the men at least two to one.

Single women.

The Women's League sponsored tonight's festivities, a fund-raiser for the children's ward at Brookline Hospital. The annual auction had become a very popular event, and every year it seemed as though the attendance, and the bids, increased.

Shane would feel much more enthusiastic about the affair if *he* wasn't one of the auction items.

Twenty firefighters from four different stations in the Boston area were up for bid tonight, selected by a vote from the entire crew. Shane figured it was payback for his bad cooking that he'd been voted in.

Dressed in a tuxedo, Captain Griffin came up from behind. Shane thought the man looked like a penguin wearing a red bow tie.

"Cummings."

"Captain."

"I expect to see some animation from you tonight," the captain said. "Last year Division 15 beat us out by two thousand dollars."

"They beat us out because they took half their clothes off and swaggered across the stage like a bunch of idiots."

"Whatever it takes." Griffin snagged a stuffed mushroom as a white-gloved waiter carrying a silver tray of hors d'oeuvres passed by. "We're going to bring in the biggest donation tonight, or someone will be on double kitchen duty his next two shifts."

Great. Win or lose, he'd be taking extra heat.

"Have a good time, son." Smiling, the captain

slapped a hand on Shane's shoulder, then headed for Sam Greenbury, another one of the four victims from Shane's crew. Sam was out of the academy only four months and brand-new to the station, so the poor bastard didn't know what he was in for.

He'd be finding out soon enough, Shane thought with a sigh. He could see the mistress of ceremonies, Doris Finwater, making her way to the podium, a sign that the auction was about to begin. Dressed in silver sequins that matched the color of her hair, Doris adjusted the height of the microphone to suit her stout, five-foot-four-inch height.

"Attention, please, attention," Doris spoke into the microphone. The band stopped playing and the roar of conversation lowered to a murmur. "Thank you so much for joining us tonight. I'm Doris Finwater, this year's Fireman's Auction coordinator."

The crowd applauded and cheered.

"As you know," Doris continued, "we have twenty firefighters here tonight who have generously offered their time to help raise money for the new wing of the Brookline Hospital children's ward. But before we begin our auction, I'd like to show everyone a short film on exactly how your generous donations will be spent and, at the same time, introduce our bachelors to you from our taped interviews."

Shane knew that was his cue to go backstage and wait until his name was called. When he came out on stage, every woman who wanted to bid would have already seen a short clip about each man. After the bidding, a limousine would take each "couple" to a restaurant, they'd have dinner, then the limo would take them home. Three, four hours tops. An easy way to make money for a good cause. He glanced at his watch. With any luck, he'd be home by eleven.

If he was really lucky, Shane thought, Captain Griffin's seventy-five-year-old mother, Fern, would win the bid. She'd lost last year by only a hundred dollars. If she did win, they'd not only be home by nine, the captain couldn't get mad at him for not bringing in enough money. Mama Fern had caught his eye in the crowd earlier and given him a thumbs-up, so Shane guessed she was determined to bid higher this year.

He hoped she won.

To the tune of "Born to Be Wild," the first bachelor was introduced and the women went wild when the bidding began.

Shane slipped a finger between his neck and his collar. It felt as if the damn shirt had shrunk. He knew that most guys would give their eyeteeth to be standing in his shoes right now—even if his shoes were too tight and too stiff. There were some fine-looking women in that crowd. It wasn't exactly a hardship to take one of them out to dinner.

But his heart just wasn't in it this year, and his mind was definitely preoccupied elsewhere.

He couldn't stop thinking about Emily. Couldn't stop thinking about the taste of her, the soft little noise she'd made when he'd kissed her. The feel of her body pressed against his. He'd picked up the phone a dozen times to call her, slammed it back down.

The sound of a woman's scream startled Shane out of his thoughts. Amid the audience's laughter, he heard Doris Finwater offer congratulations to the lucky bidder, then move on to the next bachelor. Beside him, Matt and Ken were mercilessly teasing Sam about showing some skin, and the rookie looked a bit green around the gills.

Shane shook his head at their nonsense, but did nothing to save poor Sam. While the bidding continued, he folded his hands and blocked out what was going on around him.

And against his will, his mind immediately drifted back to Emily.

He'd made the right decision about her, dammit. She deserved a hell of a lot more than he had to offer. As desperately as he wanted to see her, to be with her, to make love to her, he didn't want to hurt her.

Whatever she thought she felt for him, it was only out of gratitude. She was confused right now. Not knowing who she was or anything about herself, that would obviously mess up anyone's ability to think logically or reasonably. One day, and probably soon, she would start to remember things. Piece by piece, bit by bit, her memory would return. She'd slip back into her old life, where she belonged, and he would slip back into his.

So what was the problem? he'd asked himself a hundred times. Why not just enjoy whatever time they spent together? When it was time to go their own ways, so be it. He'd never thought ahead like this before, had never been so concerned about what was down the road.

No woman had ever made him crazy like this before, either. Completely occupied his waking thoughts, then haunted his dreams, as well. And in his dreams, he did a hell of a lot more than kiss Emily. In his dreams, he'd slipped his hands under her blouse, unhooked her bra, then filled his palms with her soft, warm flesh. In his dreams, he'd lowered his mouth and—

"Cummings." Sam tugged nervously at his bow tie. "I'm up next. What do I do?"

Sam was obviously scared to death, Shane thought, and almost felt sorry for the kid. Matt was on the stage at the moment to the tune of "Bad to the Bone." Shane rolled his eyes when he peeked from behind the curtain and watched his friend pull out a pair of sunglasses, then give his Arnold Schwarzenegger impression. The women were eating it up, and the bidding turned intense.

Shane looked back at Sam. "You know that handstand-back flip thing you did the other day at the station?"

"What about it?"

"Just do that."

"That's it?"

"That's it."

Sam seemed to relax then, and thirty seconds later he went out to the tune of "You Sexy Thing" and did a triple back flip across the stage.

And ripped his pants.

Uh-oh, Shane thought, then blew out a sigh of relief when the opening bid was five hundred, two hundred more than any other opening bid. A pair of cute twin blondes in the front were practically hyperventilating as they upped the bid. After fierce battling, the twins won Sam at a whopping three grand, the highest bid for the evening.

Still, Division 40 was in the lead by four thousand, Shane computed. The odds of him bringing in more than that were very, very slim.

Captain Griffin was going to make his life hell.

With a sigh, Shane smoothed the front of his tux, heard Doris call his name, then groaned at his music, a fast country-western song, ''Be My Baby Tonight.''

Great. What was he supposed to do with that?

He plastered a smile on his face, stepped on stage to a flurry of cheers and applause, then did the first thing that came to his mind.

He grabbed Doris.

While John Michael Montgomery wailed about love at first sight, Shane did a tricky two-step with the startled mistress of ceremonies, then kissed her cheek and released her. The crowd exploded with cheers and catcalls.

Flushed, Doris opened the bid herself at seven hundred.

Eight hundred.

One thousand.

Fifteen hundred.

C'mon, Mama Fern, Shane urged silently.

And it inched upward quickly, over two, then three thousand. Mama Fern dropped off at thirty-five hundred.

Thirty-six.

Thirty-seven.

Shane thought for a moment that was where it

would stay, when a woman called out from the back of the room.

"Five thousand dollars."

There were gasps throughout the crowd.

Five thousand dollars? That was the highest bid of the night by two thousand. Shane glanced out to see who'd made such a generous bid, but the glare from the stage lights was too great to see past the front row of people.

"We have five thousand dollars," Doris sputtered into the microphone. "Do I hear six?"

It seemed as if the entire room held its collective breath.

"Going once…going twice…sold!" Doris brought her gavel down on the podium and looked out over the sea of people. "To…?"

"Emily Barone."

At the sound of her voice, Shane felt his pulse race. Emily? Emily was *here?*

An excited murmur buzzed through the room. Most everyone in Boston knew who Emily Barone was, especially in this room full of wealthy socialites. Shane watched as she moved awkwardly through the crowd, then lifted her gaze to his.

She'd done something to her hair, he realized. It wasn't exactly shorter, it had just been cut to frame her face in soft, wispy strands. Her lips were brushed glossy red, her eyelids a subtle smoky-blue. She wore a black dress, long and sleek, cut in a low V. A string of pearls circled the base of her throat and she carried a black beaded shawl and small black purse in her hand.

If it hadn't been stuck to the top of his mouth, his tongue would have fallen out.

He heard the whispering. "Barone family"… "poisoned gelato"…"sex scandal." And he knew that she heard, as well.

Her stride appeared steady, but when their eyes met, he saw the hesitation there.

"Miss Barone," Doris said with a beaming smile. "Perhaps you'd like to come up here and claim your date for the evening."

And then suddenly she didn't look so confident. He noticed a falter in her step as she glanced around the crowded room, saw that everyone was staring at her. He saw her shoulders stiffen and her eyes widen. He was certain she was about to turn and run.

Oh, hell.

He jumped off the stage, scooped her up in his arms and carried her through the mass of people.

The room exploded with applause and laughter and cheers. Cameras flashed.

He kept going, down the carpeted hall, through the lobby, to the outside drive where the limos were lined up for the event. He opened the back door of the first limo, set Emily on the black leather bench, then slid in beside her.

The driver rolled down the window separating the front from the back. From his inside pocket, Shane pulled out the envelope containing the name of the restaurant and directions, handed it to the driver, then closed the partition window himself and turned back to Emily.

She'd pulled her shawl completely over her head and sat stiff as a post.

Smiling, he lifted one end of the shawl, then folded it back from her face. Her eyes were squeezed closed.

"You must think I'm such an idiot," she whispered.

"Why in the world would I think that?"

"For being such a coward." She turned her head away. "If you hadn't picked me up when you did, I think my knees might have given out."

"Hey." He cupped her chin in his hand and turned her face back to his. With the shawl still draped over her head, her face had an angelic quality about it. Her skin felt warm and smooth. Her scent, subtle but distinctly feminine, drew him in closer. "It took guts to walk in that room by yourself. And you just donated five thousand dollars to charity. That hardly makes you an idiot."

Still she didn't open her eyes. "Would you ask the driver to take me to my apartment?" She recited her address.

"We have dinner reservations at L'Espalier. Aren't you hungry?"

Emily felt herself leaning into Shane's touch, felt her bones melting. She snapped her spine straight again.

"No." She could still feel everyone's eyes on her at the auction, could hear the whispers. When she'd remembered the flyer she'd seen at the fire station, then decided to go and bid on Shane, she'd thought she'd been ready to face all those people. Obviously she hadn't.

She heard him sigh, then pick up the back seat phone and give the driver her address.

When he hung up, Emily opened her eyes and met Shane's intense gaze. A few more minutes and this humiliation would be over, she told herself. But first she owed him an apology.

"Shane, I'm so sorry," she began. "I knew my family was a little high-profile right now, but I hadn't realized how much so until I saw the expressions on everyone's faces tonight. And all those cameras flashing when you carried me out of that room. I can only imagine how the newspapers will twist a story like that."

"Does that matter to you?" he asked quietly. "What the newspapers might say, or people might think?"

She shook her head. "I don't care what they say about me, but now I've dragged you into the eye of the Barone hurricane, too. That's hardly a way to repay you for everything you've done for me."

"Emily." Shane lowered the shawl covering her head to the back of her neck, then gripped the ends. "I think it's time we were honest with each other."

Here it comes, she thought. The "you're-a-nice-girl-and-I-like-you-a-lot-but" speech.

"You don't have to say it, Shane," she said evenly. "I understand you aren't as attracted to me as I am to you and it's all right. Really."

He sighed heavily. "Emily—"

"And based on what's going on in my family right now," she rushed on, "not to mention the little fact that I've lost my memory, I certainly wouldn't blame you for wanting to stay as far away as possible from—''

''Emily, for God's sake, will you just shut up?''

He yanked on the shawl around her neck and pulled her closer, then his mouth slammed down on hers. She sucked in a breath at the hard press of his lips on hers, then curled her hands around the lapels of his tux jacket.

This kiss was nothing at all like the tender kiss they'd shared on the beach. This time his mouth assaulted her senses, made her forget everything but him. She knew the limo was moving through downtown traffic, heard the distant sound of a horn and the buzz of passing cars. She knew that the driver was just on the other side of the partition, too, that at any moment it might slide down and he'd see them.

She just didn't care.

Heat simmered her blood, raced through her veins. Her head spun. Wave after wave of pleasure washed through her. His mouth was relentless, demanding, and she pressed closer to him, wanting more.

Thankfully, he complied.

He deepened the kiss, slanted his mouth against hers again and again. The wild beating of her heart drowned out every thought, every doubt, every hesitation. Need vibrated through her, had her circling his neck with her arms and pressing closer still.

Then suddenly he dragged his mouth from hers. His breathing was as ragged as hers, his voice tight as he said, ''I think that tells you how I feel about you, Emily.''

He swooped down on her again before she could

respond, his mouth hot and hungry and urgent. She met him eagerly, heard the sound of her own moan as he pressed her back against the seat. The scent of leather and man filled her senses. His hands slid down her arms, skimmed the sides of her breasts, then moved upward again to cup her face.

Once again, he broke the kiss and stared down at her. His expression was dark, his eyes narrowed with desire. Pleasure, as intense as it was primitive, streaked through her.

"And another thing," he said hoarsely, "I didn't stay away from you because of what the newspapers or gossipmongers are spouting about your family. I stayed away because I've wanted you from the moment you looked at me in that ambulance. It might as well have been a bolt of lightning, it hit me so damn hard."

She blinked, trying to make sense of his words. "You...wanted me?"

He smiled at her surprise. "I've had one hell of a tough time keeping my hands off you, Emily."

"You didn't have to. I—" She hesitated, felt the heat rush to her cheeks. "I want your hands on me."

His eyes glinted in the semidarkness, then his gaze dropped to her mouth. For one heart-stopping moment she thought he was going to kiss her again.

But he didn't. Instead, he released her, then sat back against the seat and sighed. "Emily, you've just been through a major trauma. I know you're grateful to me for—"

"Is that what you think?" The heat that had been rushing through her veins cooled, settled into an icy lump in her stomach. "That I want you to kiss me, to make love to me, because I'm *grateful?*"

A muscle jumped in his jaw. "I just think you need a little more time."

"Everyone seems to have an opinion on what they think I need." Her voice was as tight as the damn teddy she'd bought to wear beneath this dress. "Not one person has asked me what I *want*."

"Emily—"

"I'm not a child, Shane." Two weeks of pent-up frustration bubbled to the surface. "I've lost my memory, not my ability to think or make my own decisions."

"For God's sake, will you just—"

The limo pulled up in front of her apartment and she opened the door before the driver could get out of the car.

"Thank you again for coming to my rescue, Mr. Cummings." She grabbed her purse from the seat. "If you don't mind, I'd prefer to see myself up."

She slammed the door and made her way up the walk, through the front entrance of her apartment, then up the stairs. She had no idea how the old Emily would have handled this mess, but the new Emily refused to let herself fall apart, refused to feel sorry for herself, and she sure as hell refused to cry.

She let herself into her apartment, tossed her shawl and purse on the chair and headed for the kitchen, hopping from foot to foot as she yanked off her new high heels and dropped them on the floor.

So much for her night of seduction, she thought, opening her cupboard. She pulled out a box of Godiva

candy her mother had sent over, opened it, then un-
wrapped a square of solid chocolate and popped it in
her mouth.

She felt better already.

She was reaching for a second piece when she
heard the knock at the door. Her pulse jumped, then
she heard a second, louder knock.

"Emily, open up," she heard Shane say from the
other side.

Frowning, she walked back to the door, picking up
her high heels on the way. If he apologized, she swore
she'd bean him with the shoes.

"Yes?" she said politely when she opened the
door, then gasped when he stepped quickly inside and
grabbed hold of her shoulders.

His mouth was set into a thin, tight line. His eyes
met hers with the heat of a laser.

"What do you want?" he asked her, tightening his
hold on her arms. "Tell me what you want."

She met and held his intense gaze, then lifted her
chin. "You," she said evenly, surely. "I want you."

Seven

Without looking back, Shane closed the door behind him and turned the latch. They both stood there, no more than a foot separating them, their eyes locked on each other.

She waited.

Anticipation heightened her senses. The sweet scent of flowers drifted from the vase on her coffee table. She heard the steady *tick-tock* from a library clock on the wall, and the sound of her own heart slamming against her ribs.

She thought if Shane didn't say something, didn't *do* something soon, her knees might give out.

When he reached for her, even before his hand touched hers, she shivered.

"Did I tell you how beautiful you look tonight?" He brought her fingers to his mouth. "Sexy."

"Thank you." Her voice was barely audible. "So do you."

Lifting one brow, he glanced down at her.

"You look handsome, I mean," she said. Then she added, "And sexy."

Smiling, he turned his attention back to her hand, lightly brushed his lips over each knuckle. "Thanks."

He closed the distance between them by maybe two inches, turned her hand over and pressed his mouth to her palm. A current of electric heat sizzled up her arm, then shot straight down to her toes.

Her shoes slipped from her hand and landed with a thud.

"You—" she had to catch her breath when the tip of his tongue touched the most sensitive spot on her palm "—you dance very well, too."

He chuckled at that, but did not look up. "I improvised."

"I think I made a few enemies tonight." With Shane still stroking her palm with his tongue, Emily had to concentrate to string together enough words to form a coherent sentence. "There was an elderly woman with blue hair who nearly tackled me when I bid on you."

"That's Fern Griffin, the captain's mother. She's got a thing for me."

Emily knew that Shane was teasing, but the truth was, what female between the ages of eight and eighty wouldn't have a thing for him? Emily had watched the faces of the women who'd been bidding on Shane. He'd made every woman laugh when he'd grabbed Doris and danced with her, and every woman sigh when he'd kissed her cheek.

And right now, Emily thought as Shane moved his lips up her hand to nibble on her wrist, he was turning her insides into liquid heat.

Had anyone ever done this to her before? she wondered. Made her heart flutter and her stomach turn upside down? She couldn't imagine that any other man could have made her feel this.

But whatever her past had been, she knew it didn't matter. The only thing that mattered was being here now, with Shane. To her, he would be her first, and the thought aroused her all the more.

"The driver," she whispered.

Sliding a hand around her waist, he pulled her body against his. "I sent him home."

"Oh."

"If you don't want me to stay," he murmured as he lowered his head to her neck, "if you have any doubts, you need to tell me."

"I—" She drew in a breath when he nipped just below her ear. "I want you to stay."

"Good." She felt his smile against her throat. "Because I have plans for you, Emily."

She slipped her hands up his chest and melted into him. "What plans?"

"Everything I've fantasized since I've met you."

"Fantasies?" Her heart tripped. "About me?"

"No, about Doris Finwater." When she tilted her head back and lifted one brow, he grinned at her. "Of course about you."

The realization that he'd been thinking about her

that way sent shimmering waves of heat through Emily's veins.

"Do you want me to tell you?" His mouth blazed kisses up her neck to her ear. "Or shall I show you?"

Her breasts grew heavy, her nipples tightened and ached. Every nerve in her body vibrated with need. A burning ache grew between her legs.

Tell me was her first thought, but she didn't think she could stand much more. Indeed, she was certain she'd come apart if he kept talking to her in that deep, seductive voice.

"Show me," she breathed.

He brought his mouth to hers, nibbled at the corner, then murmured, "You taste like chocolate."

"Godiva," she managed to say between breaths.

"Lady Godiva." He traced her lower lip with the tip of his tongue as he slid his hands down, then he cupped her buttocks and pulled her intimately against him. "But you're wearing too many clothes, I think."

You're killing me, she wanted to say, but her mind was reeling and the words simply wouldn't come. The press of his arousal at the junction of her thighs made it impossible to think, excited her beyond anything she could imagine. When he slipped his tongue inside her mouth, she heard the sound of her own moan, felt as if each cell in her body had come gloriously alive.

Rising on her toes, she moved into him, into the kiss, and met the slow but steady thrust of his tongue with her own. His hands gently squeezed her behind, then moved up her back. Emily heard the quiet rasp of her zipper opening, felt the cool air on her bare skin as the fabric slowly parted. When his fingers touched the undergarment she wore, he stilled.

"What's this?" he said against her lips, then lifted his head to gaze down at her.

"You want me to tell you?" she whispered. "Or show you?"

One corner of his mouth curved. "Show me."

Though her legs were trembling, she stepped back, then slipped the straps of her dress from her shoulders. Silk slid down her body and pooled at her feet.

Her knees might have given out right then if not for the fierce, raw look of desire that flared in Shane's eyes and held her captive. At this moment, even if her life depended on it, Emily knew she wouldn't be able to move.

With all the blood drained from his head, Shane could only stare at Emily. A black lace teddy cupped her breasts and hugged her slender waist, while an arrow of satin shot straight down to a narrow V between her legs. If his throat hadn't closed up, he swore he would have swallowed his tongue.

He couldn't count the times he'd imagined her like this, her dark eyes glazed with passion, her lips swollen and damp from his kisses. But his fantasies hadn't even come close to the reality. He wasn't prepared for the shattering devastation to his senses.

He let his hungry gaze feast on her, watched the shallow rise and fall of her breasts, the strain of lace against her soft flesh. How trite it seemed to tell her she was beautiful when she was so much more, he thought.

So he'd show her.

He reached out, felt her quiver when he slipped a thin black strap off one shoulder, then the other. The heat of her smooth skin under his fingertips, the scent of her, aroused him all the more. He slid his hands down to her waist, kept his gaze locked with hers as he inched upward, then filled his palms with her breasts. Her eyes narrowed and darkened. When he rubbed his thumbs over her hardened nipples, she caught her lower lip between her teeth.

He dipped his head.

Her arms slid over his shoulders when his mouth closed over cool lace and hot skin. Her head fell back, and when he suckled the sweet pearled bud, she moaned.

"Shane...I can't..." She sucked in a breath when he moved to her other breast. "I have to..."

He understood, knew exactly what she was trying to say. And he knew if he didn't get her in a bed soon, he'd take her right here on her glossy hardwood floor.

For the second time that night, he scooped her up in his arms. "Bedroom," he rasped.

"Through the hall, to the right." Her arms slid around his neck. Her mouth found his neck, and she rained kisses up his jaw.

Moonlight streamed through the window, shone like a beacon onto the four-poster bed. Even before he let her body slide down his, her hands were busy with the buttons of his shirt. He had to release her to get his tuxedo jacket off, and she took advantage by sliding her hands under his opened shirt, then dropping her mouth to his bare chest.

"Emily, wait," he ground out, struggling to catch his breath.

I can't wait, she thought, but was too busy, too enthralled with the hard planes and angles of his body to find her voice. I've already waited too long for you.

A lifetime, she was certain.

His muscles rippled under her fingers while he fought with the cuffs of his shirt and toed off his shoes. She nipped at his hot skin while she unbuttoned his trousers. He tasted like salt and man and desire. When she slid her tongue down his belly at the same time she tugged down his zipper, he swore, then jerked his shirt off and wrapped his arms around her.

They tumbled to the bed and rolled.

His mouth swooped down on hers, his kiss demanding and urgent. She slid her arms over his strong shoulders, raked her nails over his skin, then up over his scalp. Heat coursed through her veins, raced through her body.

She whimpered when his mouth left hers, then drew in a sharp breath when he made his way down her neck, then moved lower still. He kneaded her swollen flesh with his hands, kissed the hardened tip of each aching breast. When she was certain she could stand no more, he slid one hand down her belly and cupped her.

"Shane..." Her hands tightened on his head. "Oh, my—"

He opened the snap between her legs, pushed away the lace, then dipped into the wet heat of her body. She burst into flames.

"Your pants," she gasped.

He stripped off the rest of his clothes, then rose over her, tugged lace and satin up her body, over her head, then tossed it aside as he moved between her legs. She reached for him and surged upward as he drove himself inside her.

On a gasp, her eyes flew open in shock.

Shane went very, very still.

She was a virgin.

He lifted his head and stared at her in disbelief.

"Emily, wait, I— Dammit, I hurt you. Just don't move, okay? Just stay—"

"You didn't hurt me."

He swore when she arched her hips upward.

"Don't do that. Just—"

"I'm fine, Shane," she whispered, and thrust her hips upward again, causing him to break out in a sweat. "I'm fine. I'm wonderful."

"Emily—"

"Don't stop." She wrapped her arms and legs tightly around him and held him close. "Please, Shane, don't stop. Not now."

Jaw clenched, he groped for even the tiniest bit of control, but then she reared upward again, forcing him to move with her, inside her, and it was impossible to think about anything but the hot, tight fit of her body and the desperate need to mate.

"Shane, this is… Oh, my—"

He watched her eyes open in shock as the first shudder rocked through her. Though his own body screamed for release, he held back, reveling in watching her pleasure. She arched upward on a moan, taking him more deeply as the flame burst to life, then swept through her like a firestorm. She writhed under him, completely lost to the pleasure. He felt every tremor, every sharp intake of breath, every wild, frantic beat of her heart.

Muscles straining, breathing ragged, he stilled until she floated back to him, but then her eyes, still glazed with desire, met his and he began to move again, hard and fast. Arms clutching his shoulders, legs wrapped tightly around his, she moved with him, eagerly met every thrust, until he felt his own climax slam into him. He groaned, a ragged, primitive sound that tore through his senses and resonated in his blood and his brain.

Spent, he rolled to his side and gathered her close.

It took several minutes before Emily could find her voice, before she could even move. Eyes closed, she lay in Shane's arms, her hand splayed on his broad chest. She felt as if she were on his sailboat again, gently gliding over the peaceful sea. She heard the steady, deep thud of his heart against her ear and the sound calmed her own racing heart.

"Emily," he said quietly, breaking the stillness. "I'm not sure what to say. I've never— I mean, that was the first time that I— Oh, hell."

She smiled when he dragged a hand through his hair and swore again. It helped to know that he'd been thrown off balance, too. But she was too happy, feeling too wonderful, to let her mood be dimmed. "Why, Shane," she said, stroking his chest with her fingertips, "are you trying to tell me that was your first time, too?"

"Emily, for crying out loud." On a sigh, he rolled her to her back and gazed down at her. "You know what I mean."

She touched his cheek with her hand. "If it will ease your conscience any, I'm just as surprised as you are. Since there were birth control pills in my medicine cabinet, well, I'd sort of assumed that I'd…done this before." Holding his gaze, she whispered, "Just don't tell me you're sorry, Shane. Please don't tell me that."

He covered her hand with his, then turned his lips to her palm. "I'm not sorry. I would have been more careful if I'd known, but I'm definitely not sorry."

Relief poured through her. She felt gloriously content and suddenly very curious. "Is it always as wonderful as this?" she asked, still too exhilarated to be embarrassed by such an intimate question.

He lifted a brow. "Are you looking for an evaluation?"

"Absolutely."

She gasped when he suddenly rolled to his back, bringing her with him to rest on top of his chest. "Miss Barone, I can say unequivocally, without a doubt, that you have achieved a level as close to excellence as humanly possible. Any closer, you'd be calling the paramedics to revive me."

She knew he was teasing, but his answer still delighted her. Sliding her leg over his, she pressed her mouth to his chest and tasted the salty dampness still on his skin.

"So you're telling me that it doesn't get any better than that?" she murmured. "That there's no need to—" she moved one hand down his flat belly, felt his muscles jerk under her touch "—practice?"

He moaned when her hand slid lower, then drew in a sharp breath when she stroked the hard length of him. His hips moved, then he reached for her shoulders and suddenly she was on her back again.

"Do me a favor," he said roughly as he stared down at her. "Just don't call the paramedics from my station."

Emily woke a little while later in a tangle of sheets and man. One of Shane's legs lay casually over hers and his arm was draped across her waist. After he'd made love to her the second time, she'd fallen asleep on her back, and he'd dozed off on his stomach.

She'd had no idea making love was so...exerting.

She glanced over at him, watched the play of moonlight on his handsome face, then slid her gaze down the length of his bare body. He looked like a statue of a Greek god. Muscled arms, chiseled face, powerful legs. And the similarities didn't end there, she thought, dropping her gaze to a part of his anatomy she couldn't see at the moment, but now knew quite well.

Her cheeks actually burned as she wished he'd roll over.

What a wonderful, incredible lover he'd been. Tender, passionate, spontaneous. The kind of lover women dreamed about, longed for. And tonight he'd been hers.

She didn't want to think about—or worry about—tomorrow, or any day after that. Hadn't she already learned it was impossible to know what tomorrow held? She wanted only to think about *this* night. She would cherish every moment they'd shared.

Carefully she slid out from under him, hesitating when he shifted on the bed, then crept out of the bedroom and into the bathroom. Flipping on the light, she moved to the mirror over her sink. Her new hairstyle was a bit askew, her face flushed, her lips still swollen from Shane's kisses.

"Emily." She said her own name out loud, amazed at the familiar sound of her own voice.

For the first time since her accident, she felt as if she knew the woman staring back at her from the mirror. This is who I am, she thought, touching her fingers to her lips and smiling. She no longer felt like a blank slate. It no longer even mattered that she couldn't remember her past, or if she would ever remember.

She felt like a babe who'd just been born, naked and trembling, freed from the confines of nothingness into bright colors and thunderous sounds. It was exciting. It was frightening. It was stimulating.

She considered slipping back into bed with Shane—no, *jumping* back into bed with him—but instead she snatched her robe from the back of her bathroom door and headed for the kitchen. They'd missed their dinner reservations and she knew he'd be hungry when he woke. She could have ordered something in, but she had a sudden, overwhelming desire to cook. She had no idea what she would make, but instinct

Eight

Shane woke to the scent of garlic and herbs. He reached for Emily, but the rumpled sheets beside him were cold. Frowning, he raised his head from the pillow and glanced at the clock on the nightstand: 11:40 p.m. He'd only been out about thirty or forty minutes, he realized, then sat on the edge of the bed and dragged a hand through his hair.

Whatever she was cooking, he hoped she had enough for two.

He pulled on his trousers and found his way to the kitchen, then leaned against the doorjamb and watched her. Dressed in a short blue robe, she stood at the stove, stirring a bubbling pot of sauce.

Witch's brew, he thought, for surely she'd bewitched him tonight. Used her magic to turn him inside out and upside down. What else could possibly explain what had happened to him—to both of them—tonight?

He thought he should feel some remorse, even a small bit of guilt, that he'd taken her virginity. But he didn't. The fact was, he felt an almost primitive sense of pleasure that he had been her first lover. That no man before him had touched her the way he had. He'd wanted her, she'd wanted him. They were both adults. Simple enough.

Only it wasn't simple, he thought, studying her as she scooped up a spoonful of sauce and tasted. It definitely wasn't simple.

And that was what made him most uneasy of all.

"Smells good."

At the sound of his voice she turned and gave him a smile, part shy, part coquette, that made his breath hitch.

"It's not exactly L'Espalier," she said, turning back to the stove, "but I assumed you'd be hungry."

"Starving."

He pushed away from the doorjamb and moved behind her, then slid his arms around her waist and pulled her close. She leaned back against him and sighed when he pressed his lips to the side of her neck. "You okay?" he asked carefully.

Smiling, she turned her head to look up at him. "I'd say I'm better than okay."

"Yeah." He grinned back at her. "Me, too."

Her cheeks blossomed to a lovely pink, and she turned quickly back to her sauce. "There's an open bottle of wine on the counter, if you'd—" she drew in a breath when he traced the curve of her ear with the tip of his tongue "—like some."

"Sure." He tasted the softness of her lobe with his lips. The breath she'd drawn in shuddered out. She released the wooden spoon, then put her hands on his hips to steady herself.

"Ah, glasses are in the…cupboard…to the right of the sink."

"Okay." He slid his hands up and cupped the softness of her breasts through the thin cotton robe she wore.

"Or if you just want a soda," she breathed, closing her eyes, "I have regular or diet, or—"

He turned her in his arms and kissed her slowly, tenderly, until they were both struggling to breathe and he knew she needed more time. He wanted to drag her back to bed, but he knew she needed a little more time before he made love to her again. Mentally, emotionally, physically, what had happened between them tonight was completely new to her.

And to himself, he realized.

But he wasn't ready to deal with any of those feelings right now. He was still too out of balance, still too unnerved by the intensity of what had happened between them.

In spite of the heat surging through his blood, he knew he needed to back off. Put a little distance between them for the moment.

It took a will of iron, but he finally managed to release her and step away. "I'll get the wine."

He poured two glasses, set one down for her beside the stove, then leaned back against the counter and watched her while she worked. "You look as if you've done this a time or two," he said, sipping his wine.

"I guess I have." She turned the heat off under the bubbling sauce, then moved to the cupboard, pulled out two plates and filled them with pasta from a strainer in the sink. "My kitchen is well-stocked, and it feels comfortable to me to be at the stove. How it tastes is another story."

Strange, he thought, that it felt comfortable to be here with her, as well. That watching her fuss about the kitchen in her robe, with her hair tumbling around that glorious neck, her cheeks flushed and the haze of passion still lingering in her eyes, was as natural to him as breathing. And arousing, he mused, letting his gaze skim down to where creamy white thighs met the hem of her robe. The idea that she was naked under that robe made him instantly hard, and he was glad when she instructed him to sit at the table.

"Be honest." She worried her bottom lip as she placed a steaming plate of spaghetti in front of him, then sat down beside him. "If it's too spicy, we can always order pizza."

It was spicy, but wonderfully so. The sauce was a creamy tomato, with ground sausage and mushrooms. The rich, robust flavor exploded in his mouth.

Damn.

"It *is* too spicy," she said when he didn't speak. "I knew it. We'll order a pizza. Tell me what kind you like and I'll just—"

He grabbed her hand and pulled her back to the table when she started to stand. "Emily, for God's sake, give me a second. I'm having a reverent moment here, just let me savor it.''

"You like it?"

"Like it?" He forked up another big bite, shoveled it in and groaned. "My God, woman, I think I just died and went to heaven."

Smiling with pleasure, she sat back down and picked up her glass of wine. "Maria told me I was a good cook, but I wasn't certain if she was just being nice."

"Maria?"

"My cousin." Emily took a bite of pasta. "She came over the other day to see how I was. I didn't remember her, though she did seem familiar somehow. She's the first person who's been completely honest with me about what's happening in my family, the photos of my cousin Gina in the tabloids, then the tainted gelato, and of course, the link to the Mafia, which Maria says would be laughable if people weren't so quick to believe what they hear and read. I have to admit, it is all a little overwhelming. Oh, and then there's the curse on top of all that, too.''

Shane actually stopped eating for a moment. "What curse?"

"It started more than sixty years ago," Emily said. "My grandfather, Marco Barone, had been engaged to his godfather's daughter, Lucia Conti, but on Valentine's Day my grandfather eloped with my grandmother, Angelica, instead. The two families have been feuding ever since, and to top it off, young Lucia put a so-called 'Valentine's Day Curse' on my grandparents and all their descendants.''

Shane lifted a brow. "And your family believes in this curse?"

With a shrug, Emily reached for her wine again. "According to Maria, some do, some don't, but there's no question that some strange things have happened on that date, most tragic of all, my grandmother's miscarriage of her first child on their first anniversary. And then most recently, the gelato debacle. That was on Valentine's Day, too."

Shane shook his head. "That's life, Emily. All you have to do is turn on the TV or pick up a newspaper to know that. Nobody has control over any of it. It just happens."

Emily was quiet for a moment, sipping her wine while she watched Shane eat. She'd seen a flicker of something in his eyes before he turned his attention back to his food. Pain? Anger? Had he been thinking of his own family? she wondered. He'd lost both his parents, much too soon, and no one had put a curse on his family.

He was right, she thought. It certainly did no good to sit around worrying about what might happen. Life was what was happening now. Life was sitting here at this table, eating pasta at midnight after making wonderful, spectacular love.

The memory of that still hummed over her skin.

"So tell me, Shane," she said, lifting her glass to her lips nonchalantly. "Who was the lucky girl last year?"

His fork halted halfway to his mouth. "What?"

She nearly laughed at the expression of complete

surprise on his face. "The auction last year. Who was the lucky winner?"

"Oh. Ah, her name was Aurel."

"That's an unusual name. What was her last name?"

"I haven't a clue." He turned his attention back to his food. "She just called herself Aurel."

"Really." Emily truly hadn't meant to utter the word with such disdain. It just sort of slipped out. "Does she live here in Boston?"

"She lives in New York." He reached for the bottle of Chianti sitting on the table. "Wine?"

"No, thank you." But she did sip at the small amount still in her glass. "Did she come to Boston for the auction?"

"No." He filled his own glass and took a swig. "She was working a fashion show here in Boston."

"A fashion show?" She glanced up, then quickly composed herself and casually swirled the wine in her glass. "So she's a model?"

"Last I heard. Sure you don't want some more wine?"

Shaking her head, Emily set her glass on the table, then picked up her fork and pushed her spaghetti around her plate. "Did you have a nice time?"

"It was fine."

Fine? What was that supposed to mean? Fine, as in *fine,* or fine, as in okay? She had to bite the inside of her lip to keep herself from asking any more questions.

After a long, silent moment, Shane pushed his now-empty plate aside and leaned closer. "We went to dinner at The Oak Room, then the limo took us back to her hotel. I walked her to her door, said good-night, gave her a kiss on the cheek and left. We did not sleep together.''

She nearly choked at his bluntness. "I was *not* asking you that!''

"Not in words,'' he said, cocking his head. "But I can see the little wheels turning. You're thinking that because you and I slept together, that I slept with Aurel, too.''

Straightening her back and shoulders, Emily took a bite of pasta. "It's none of my business. I apologize for prying.''

Chuckling, he reached across the table and took her chin in his hand. "She was a sweet, but very ditzy blonde from the Bronx who referred to herself in the third person and thought she had an acting career ahead of her because she'd been on a television dating show. She also believed in the existence of a parallel universe, and in excruciating detail described to me her other life on the planet Nathra where she was a recording artist under the name of Lexandra. All this information had been channeled to her by a guide called Blunther.''

She blinked. "How…interesting.''

"Emily,'' he said with a sigh, "I'm no saint. I've dated a lot of women, though I certainly haven't slept with nearly as many as you might think.'' He stroked her cheek with his thumb. "But what happened here tonight between you and me was different. It wasn't casual. It meant something. You got that?''

She nodded, felt her pulse jump when he leaned closer and brushed her mouth with his.

"Tell me," he murmured against her lips.

"It meant something," she whispered, and believed it.

He kissed her, gently at first, until the heat built up again, making her heart pound and her body ache with need. He pulled her to his lap and she straddled him, then he unknotted the belt at her waist and slid his hands inside to cup her breasts. Breathless, she slid her arms around his neck, let her head fall back on a moan when he entered her, then began to move.

Holding on tightly to each other, they rushed to the cliff, teetered there for what felt like a lifetime, then together they fell over the edge.

The sound of a construction truck beeping and men's voices on the street below yanked Emily from sleep. She managed to open one eye and glance at her clock, then groaned at the time: ten o'clock. City maintenance had been working all week on a water line, and apparently Sunday would be no exception.

Burrowing deeper into the softness of the bed, she attempted to find her way back to her dream, which involved herself, Shane, a bed and very little clothing.

When the truck rattled her windows and shook her walls, she covered her head with her pillow to muffle the noise. Now where was I...?

Oh, yes, she remembered now. On her stomach. Shane had been kissing her neck, slowly working his way down her bare back with his mouth while his hands slid over her shoulders, down her sides, dipped between the mattress to cup her breasts.

How real it all seemed, she thought, then went very still as she remembered that it *had* been real.

Shane *had* spent the night with her. Made love with her. Her lips slowly curved. It didn't matter that her body ached and her senses were dulled. She felt wonderful. Glorious.

And just a little bit wicked.

She pulled her head out from under the pillow and her smile faded as she glanced at the bed beside her.

It was empty.

The truck on the street below rumbled away. Dragging a hand through her tousled hair, she sat and looked around the bedroom. His clothes were gone, as well. She listened for a sound from the bathroom or kitchen, but her apartment was quiet. Much too quiet.

He couldn't have been gone more than an hour or two, she thought. They'd dozed off and on during the evening, but had spent most of the night in each other's arms. It amazed her how natural it had felt to lie nestled against Shane's strong body, how completely at ease she'd been. And every time she thought she'd never move again, had to struggle to even drag a breath into her lungs, all he had to do was skim a hand over her hip or brush his lips against hers and the fire would ignite once again and burn just as hot as before.

And now he was gone.

Last night he'd told her that making love with her had meant something, that it wasn't casual. She'd be-

lieved him, but she wasn't so foolish to think that
because he'd wanted to make love with her he was
looking for a relationship, either. Especially a permanent one.

Could she be content with anything less? she wondered, running a hand over the cold, rumpled sheets
beside her. She could still smell him, could still feel
him, and God help her, she missed him already.

Sighing, she slid out of bed and reached for her
robe, then headed for the bathroom. She had no idea
when she'd see him again, or even *if* she would see
him again. It hurt; she'd be lying if she told herself
it didn't. But she had no regrets, she thought as she
stepped into the shower. Whatever happened now,
last night would be a memory she would cherish always.

She showered quickly, blew her hair dry, then
pulled on a pair of fitted jeans and a pink ruffled
wraparound blouse that Maria had helped her pick
out. She changed her shoes four times before settling
on a pair of square-toed brown mules with two-inch
heels.

Not bad, she thought as she studied her new look
in her mirrored closet doors. She might not remember
who she was before, but she was beginning to like
and be comfortable with who she was now. She was
ready to make new memories, new experiences. She
was hoping that somehow Shane would continue to
be a part of those memories and new experiences, but
she wouldn't push and she sure as hell wouldn't beg.

Who knows, she thought with a smile as she fluffed

her new hairstyle, maybe Shane would be the one begging.

Laughing at the ridiculous idea, she grabbed her purse and headed for her front door. She was going out, and she didn't have a clue where. Just... wherever. It was a beautiful day. Maybe she'd take one of those city tours, or go to a museum or an art gallery. Boston was rich with history and culture. She'd learn it all over again. The idea excited her, had her throwing her door open wide.

Then shrieking in alarm.

A man dressed in a white shirt and navy slacks stood in her doorway, his fist lifted and poised to knock.

"Joseph Barone!" Emily clapped a hand to her chest. "You scared the hell out of me! For God's sake, you could have—"

She stopped, realized what she'd just said, then pressed a hand to her mouth and stared. She couldn't move. Couldn't breathe.

"Emily?" Joseph furrowed his brow. "Are you all right?"

"I—I remember you." Her words tumbled out on a shaky breath. "You're Joseph Barone. My cousin."

"You're white as a sheet." He stepped inside, closed the door behind him, then took her by the arm. "Come sit down."

"You don't understand." Her heart pounded wildly as he pulled her to the sofa and made her sit. "I *know* who you are. I haven't recognized anyone since my accident, not even my own mother and father, but Joseph, I know you. I wasn't even trying, I didn't have time, and then suddenly there you were and—''

''Emily, stop.'' He sat beside her, took her hand in his and rubbed her icy fingers. ''Slow it down for a minute. You're trembling.''

Her pulse racing, Emily drew in a breath, then slowly released it.

''Okay. Now, let's try it again,'' he said evenly. ''You opened the door and knew who I was.''

She nodded.

''What else do you remember?''

''I—'' She struggled to think, then touched her fingers to the sudden throbbing in her temple and whispered, ''Nothing.''

''Are you sure?'' he coaxed.

''Only what my mother told me,'' she said with a sigh. ''You're the CFO at Baronessa. You're thirty-three and you rarely come to family get-togethers since your wife died.'' Emily closed her eyes. ''Oh, God, Joseph, I'm so sorry. I shouldn't have said that.''

''It's been five years, Emily,'' he said quietly. ''It's all right.''

But it wasn't, she knew. She'd seen the brief flash of pain in his hazel eyes. Losing someone you loved was never truly all right. It just was.

When he squeezed her hand to reassure her, it felt as if a camera had flashed in her head. First a bright, blinding light, then an image. ''Arm wrestling,'' she blurted out.

He frowned at her. ''What?''

''I—I'm outside…at a park, I think. I'm just a

child. You're arm wrestling at a table with another guy!'' she said excitedly. "Everyone is cheering."

"Arm wrestling at a park?" He stared at her for a long moment with a blank look, then lifted his brow in surprise. "Good grief, that was twelve years ago. At Claudia's sweet sixteen party. It was at Longwood Cricket Club. My friend and I got into trouble from both our mothers for knocking a pitcher of red punch all over Claudia's white dress. She screamed so loud in my ear she nearly broke my eardrum."

Emily laughed, then closed her eyes and concentrated, trying to force the image back, to recall even one more tiny detail, but her mind refused to cooperate. Shaking her head, she opened her eyes again on a sigh. "That's it."

"It's a start for now. The rest will come when it comes," he said. "There's a family reunion in July. If you haven't already remembered everything by then, I'm sure seeing everyone together will jog some more memories. For now—" he stood and tugged her up off the sofa "—per Maria's orders, I'm here to take you to lunch."

"Joseph, for heaven's sake, I appreciate the offer, but really, it's not necessary. I was just on my way out to explore Boston, maybe take a downtown tour or go to a museum."

"Perfect. I was a tour guide for college credits one summer. We'll start with Faneuil Hall, also known as the Cradle of Liberty. Built in 1742 and given to the city by Peter Faneuil," he said in a very stuffy tour guide voice. "The upper story served as a meeting hall during the Revolutionary War and was the scene of many stirring gatherings.''

Why not? Emily thought. She let him drone on about British officers' occupation of the city and how they used the hall as a theater during that time. She'd already decided she wasn't going to stay home, anyway. Why not share the afternoon with her cousin, get reacquainted with him and keep her mind off Shane at the same time? It was a good plan, she decided as Joseph led her toward his car.

Now, if only it worked.

Nine

At six o'clock that evening Shane parked his car in front of Emily's apartment building. Two apartments down, four city workers stood around an open trench in the middle of the street, watching while two other men down inside the trench shoveled dirt. A white poodle yipped at the workers as its owner, an elderly woman wearing a navy-blue dress and a straw hat, tugged at the dog's leash and dragged the still-yapping animal down the sidewalk toward Shane. Faced with a new, and much closer intruder, the dog went into a frenzy.

Shane forced a polite smile while the woman and her annoying dog passed, then made his way up Emily's walk. Inside the building, the sound of classical music drifted from one of the downstairs apartments and the smell of baking chicken filled the entryway, reminding him he hadn't eaten more than a bagel since early that morning.

At the top of the landing, he hesitated at the sound of a man's voice coming from the hallway around the corner, then at the sound of Emily's soft laugh. Frowning, he moved closer.

"I had a wonderful time today, Joseph," Shane heard Emily say. "Are you sure you don't want to come in?"

"I've got an early meeting to prepare for," the man said. "Maybe next time."

Maybe next time? Shane clenched his jaw. Who the hell was this Joseph? Her ex-boyfriend, maybe? Shane couldn't remember the guy's name, but Joseph did sound familiar. And why had Emily had a "wonderful time" with him today?

He stepped around the corner and felt a muscle jump in his jaw when he saw Emily lean forward to hug the guy, then kiss him on the cheek.

Jealousy, dark and vicious, slammed like a fist in his gut. The intensity of it shocked him, nearly had him grabbing the guy by his collar and punching his lights out.

"Shane." Emily straightened as she spotted him, and smiled cautiously. The man with her straightened as well, and he lifted one dark eyebrow as Shane met his gaze. "I...wasn't expecting you."

"I tried to call you this afternoon." Shane moved forward, kept his eyes locked with the other man, who clearly was no happier about Shane's appearance than Shane was about his. "Obviously, you were out."

Having a wonderful time.

"I went to lunch and sightseeing with Joseph." She touched the man's arm. "Joseph, this is Shane Cummings. Shane, this is Joseph Barone, my cousin."

Joseph *Barone*.

Her cousin, for God's sake. The rush of combat eased and so did the fierce need to claim the woman standing three feet away from him. Feeling like a complete idiot, Shane stepped forward and shook the man's hand.

"Shane." Joseph's grip was firm, his gaze still wary. "Emily's told me all about you."

"Is that so?" Not *all* about him, Shane was certain. If she had, Joseph would probably be the one wanting to punch some lights out.

"I told him how you found me in the plant and carried me out just seconds before the explosion," Emily said quickly. "And how you came to the hospital to visit me afterward."

"The Barones owe you a debt of gratitude." Joseph released Shane's hand. "If there's ever anything we can do for you, please let us know."

"Thanks, but it's not necessary."

Joseph glanced at Emily. "Well, if you're all right, I guess I'll run along."

"Of course I'm all right. And thank you again for a lovely day." Emily gave her cousin another hug. "You can tell Maria you accomplished your mission and that I thank her, too."

Shane watched Joseph stroll away. "Your cousin."

"Of course it was my cousin." Emily slid a look over her shoulder as she slipped her keys in the door, then opened it. "Who did you think he was?"

"Uh…" He squirmed as he followed her inside. "No one."

Emily tossed her keys and purse on an entry table and turned to face him. "You find me in the hallway with another man, hugging him, and you thought he was 'no one'?"

"Okay, so maybe I, uh…" He scratched at his neck. "Maybe I thought it was your ex-boyfriend."

"Jeffrey?" She stared at him in disbelief. "You actually thought that I'd spend the night making love with you, then go out with Jeffrey the next day?"

He was feeling more ridiculous by the second. "I didn't know what to think."

"I didn't know what to think this morning when I woke up and you were gone, either," she said quietly.

Dammit. Now he didn't just feel ridiculous, he felt like a heel. He moved toward her, put his hands on her shoulders.

"My pager went off. I was called in on a new construction fire in Newton. You were sleeping so peacefully, I didn't want to wake you."

He'd also known if he had, it would have been ten times more difficult to leave. When she just looked at him, one brow raised, he added, "Okay, I should have left a note, I realize that now. I'm sorry."

She stepped closer to him, smiled softly. "You don't have to explain yourself to me, Shane. It's all right."

She was so damn understanding that now he really did feel like a heel. "It's not all right." He slid his hands up her shoulders and cupped her face. "I care about you, Emily. Very much. All the more reason I don't want to hurt you.''

''I'm not as fragile as you and everyone else seem to think,'' she said evenly. ''If you don't want to see me again, then just say so. I won't fall apart.''

He should have felt relief at her words, but instead, he felt his temper rising. ''I never said I didn't want to see you again,'' he said irritably. ''I'm just trying to be honest with you.''

''You mean that you're not looking for any kind of relationship and you don't want to get married.'' She sighed. ''And to think I already had the invitations and dress picked out.''

She was making fun of him, dammit. Frowning, he dropped his hands from her face. ''I'm so glad you find this amusing.''

''Oh, Shane.'' She surprised him by throwing her arms around his shoulders and giving him a quick kiss. ''You're just so serious. You really need to lighten up and enjoy life a little.''

''Is that so?'' In spite of his annoyance, he slid his hands up her back and drew her closer. ''And what do you suggest I do for enjoyment?''

''Well, let's see.'' She pursed her lips together thoughtfully. ''You like to sail, so that's definitely a good choice. And they say a good book is relaxing.''

''They do, do they?'' He dipped his head to nibble on her earlobe. ''What else do they say is relaxing?''

Her breath came in short little gasps. ''Uh... numismatics.''

He eased his head away from her and lifted a dubious eyebrow.

"Coin collecting," she murmured.

Smiling, he lowered his mouth to lightly brush his lips against hers. "I think I've got a better idea."

His tongue parted her lips, then slid inside, tasting the sweetness. Her breath came quicker now, and she wound her arms tightly around his neck. He deepened the kiss and felt her shiver when he skimmed along her waist, then slipped under her pretty ruffled blouse to trace the undersides of her breasts with his knuckles. Her breath caught in her throat when he cupped her soft flesh. When he circled her hardened nipples with his thumbs, she moaned.

Blood pounded in his veins, and his own breath was hard and labored. Need clawed at him, had him wrapping his arms tightly around her waist, lifting her off the ground to carry her to the bedroom.

They both froze at the unexpected knock at the door.

He dropped his forehead to hers. "Maybe they'll go away."

The knock came again, louder. "Department of Water and Power," a man's voice said from the hallway.

On an oath, Shane released her and stepped away.

Emily drew in a breath to steady herself, then opened the door just enough to stick her head out.

"Sorry to bother you, miss." A city worker handed Emily a flyer. "But we have to shut down the water to your building. Not sure how long, anywhere from fifteen minutes up to three or four hours, but we'll come back and let you know soon as we've made our repairs. Sorry for the inconvenience."

Emily thanked the man, then closed the door and leaned back against it. Shane looked at her lips, slightly swollen and red from his kiss, and the lingering glaze of passion in her eyes.

Dammit.

"Come on," he said with a sigh, then grabbed her purse and keys and handed them to her.

"Where are we going?"

"Someplace you've never been." He slipped an arm around her waist, gave her a quick, hard kiss, then pulled her out the front door.

"You've already taken me there," she said with a grin, then laughed when he shook his head.

"I'm talking food now, Emily. And beer. Do you like beer?" he asked, leading her down the stairs.

"I don't know," she said, more than a little breathless. "But I can't wait to find out."

On a quaint, cobbled street not far from the marina, Darcy's Irish Pub sat nestled between an antique jeweler and a used-book store. A green neon sign flashed Open in the beveled glass window while an automated wooden leprechaun puppet danced beside a pot of shiny gold pieces. Fascinated, Emily read a sign over the entrance: "May you live as long as you want, and never want as long as you live!"

The sound of laughter and music spilled through the open door when a man and a woman who appeared to be in their twenties came out of the pub. The couple waved a greeting to Shane, then set out down the sidewalk, arm in arm and apparently very much in love.

"Tell me now if you'd rather go somewhere more quiet and less crowded," Shane said, holding the door open. "Once we're inside, there's no hope of escape."

Wondering what he meant by such an odd comment, Emily stepped inside and was immediately captivated. Families sat at dark wood tables eating their dinner, men and women crowded the bar area, drinking from tall, frosty mugs of beer ranging in color from amber to molasses. The ceiling was open beam, the forest green walls covered with pictures of Ireland, famous men of Irish descent and past celebrations of St. Patrick's Day at the pub. Celtic music and the mouth-watering smell of food grilling filled the air.

"Shane!" The bartender's voice boomed over the din in the pub. He was a tall, burly man with a handsome, well-weathered face and a thick crown of pewter-colored hair. "It's about damn time you showed that ugly mug of yours around here."

"You want to see ugly, Darcy O'Dougal, look in that mirror behind you." An attractive, middle-aged waitress with a lovely Irish accent and a mass of red curls passed by carrying a tray of empty beer mugs. "I may be an old broad, but Shane here still makes my heart flutter. Come here, lad, give Katie a kiss and introduce your friend to me."

Emily watched as Shane dutifully kissed the woman's cheek. "Katherine Murphy, this is Emily Barone. And that blowhard behind the bar is my uncle Darcy."

"Blowhard, am I?" Darcy scowled at his nephew.

"You're not too old to have your ears boxed, laddie, but seeing's how you've brought such a pretty lass with you today, I'll save that pleasure for later. An honor to meet you, Miss Emily Barone."

Emily was about to respond when Darcy snatched up a mug of beer from the counter and lifted it as he gave a hearty shout over the noise. "Attention, everyone! A welcome toast to Emily!"

Everyone in the place lifted a glass and shouted back, "To Emily!"

For a moment Emily was too stunned to do anything more than stare in amazement. Though the attention made her cheeks flame, she felt a comfortable warmth in her stomach, as well.

"You want the usual?" Katie asked Shane, who nodded and held up two fingers.

"Make room for my nephew and his friend." Darcy shooed two men from their bar stools, then placed two meaty fists on the bar and leaned forward when Emily and Shane sat. "What'll it be for you, Miss Emily? A pint of Guinness or something that requires less chewing?"

Emily glanced at Shane in confusion, then back to Darcy. "I don't know. Why don't you pick for me?"

"I like this lass already." Darcy pulled two mugs from a small freezer and filled them from different taps. "A woman of intellect and fine manners. Can't imagine what she's doing here with you."

"She's got amnesia and doesn't know any better," Shane said good-naturedly.

"I may box your ears yet, boy." Darcy slid the mugs across the bar, then leaned in close to Emily.

"Three-quarters of what Shane here says is lies and the other half is without any foundation of truth. You'd do best to remember that, Miss Emily."

"You gonna blither-blather all day down there?" a man from the other end of the bar hollered out. "I've got an empty mug here."

"It'll match that head of yours, Timothy Johnson," Darcy shot back.

When Timothy came back with a comment about a certain part of his anatomy that would match Darcy's face, the bar erupted into laughter, and a volley of insults ensued between the two men.

Wide-eyed, Emily stared at Shane, who merely grinned, then lifted his mug and raised it to hers.

"Cheers."

"Cheers."

She felt Shane's eyes on her as she took her first sip of beer. The beer was ice-cold, slightly bitter, but crisp. Not so bad, she thought. She turned her attention to the people around her. In the restaurant area, waitresses served platters of food family-style while a wandering magician in a yellow-plaid overcoat performed tableside tricks and made animal balloons for the children.

"You okay?" Shane leaned close and spoke into her ear. "We can sneak out now, if you want, while my uncle's back is turned, though I swear he has eyes in the back of his head and he'll probably catch us. Then he *will* box my ears."

"Well, we certainly can't have that," Emily said with a laugh. "Besides, I can't wait to see what he'll do next. He's quite colorful, isn't he?"

"That's one way to describe him." Shane looked at his uncle, who was currently arguing with a bald man over city politics. "I've heard several other descriptions, most of which I couldn't repeat."

Emily watched Shane's uncle fill four beer glasses, then one at a time slide each frosty mug down the glossy oak bar to land directly on target in front of four different patrons. All without missing a beat of his political argument.

"And how would you describe him?" she asked.

"Loud, quick-tempered, opinionated." Shane took a long pull on his beer, then looked over at his uncle. "He's got the biggest heart you'll ever see, cries like a baby at sappy movies, though he'll deny that to the death. He works like a dog, and he's always been there for me."

"And you're always there for him, too, aren't you?" she asked.

"Of course." Shane grinned. "Who else would put up with such a belligerent old coot?"

"Looks to me like Katie would," Emily said, watching as the redhead moved between the two arguing men and told Darcy to shake a leg.

"Katie?" Shane laughed at the idea. "She's worked here since I was a kid. My uncle and Katie are just friends."

Men, Emily thought with sigh. They were so clueless. What Emily saw in Katie's eyes when she looked at Darcy was definitely not friendship. Anyone could see it.

Or maybe it was just one woman in love recognizing another.

It was a foolish, dangerous thing to fall in love with Shane, Emily knew. But it wasn't as if she'd been given a choice in the matter. From the moment he'd walked into her hospital room, maybe even from the first moment he'd scooped her up in his arms and carried her out of that burning building, she'd been in love with him. Foolish or not, that was the reality.

Fortunately, her wayward thoughts were cut short when Katie brought out the food, a giant pastrami sandwich surrounded by a mountain of golden French fries. It looked and smelled wonderful, and Emily was about to take a bite when several loud groans and a burst of laughter from the back of the pub stopped her.

"What's that all about?" she asked Shane, who'd already dug into his sandwich.

Without even glancing over his shoulder, he said, "Whiskey poker."

"Whiskey poker?" She furrowed her brow. "What's that?"

"A mutated form of poker, but no money bets in the pub, just tokens that can be used here on St. Patrick's Day." Shane took a swig of beer. "Some people call it knock poker, because you knock when you think you have the best hand. The rules and stakes vary from game to game, but it's basically the same."

"What happens if you knock and you don't have the best hand?" she asked.

"Eat your sandwich, darlin'," he said with a grin. "And then I'll show you."

*   *   *

Except for the soft lap of water against the boats and gentle creaking of wood, the marina was quiet when Shane pulled into the parking lot later that night and shut off the ignition. Beside him, Emily sat with her head back against the seat and her eyes closed. If not for the smile on her lips, he might have even thought she was asleep.

Unable to resist, he leaned over and nibbled on one corner of that pretty mouth, felt her smile widen as her arms came around his neck. He traced her lips with his tongue, and when she opened to him he slid inside. She sighed with pleasure, touched her tongue to his and pulled him closer.

She tasted like key lime pie, a specialty at his uncle's pub that Katie had insisted Emily try before they'd left. He savored the tangy, sweet taste of her, but it wasn't enough. The sudden thought that it might never be enough felt like a claw in his gut, but he shrugged the feeling off. It would *have* to be enough, he told himself.

He eased away from her, brushed his thumb over her damp lips. "If I don't stop kissing you right now, marina security is going to have a real show when they make their rounds."

"I've never been anyone's show before," Emily said breathlessly. "At least, I don't think I have."

"There are some firsts that you're better off not experiencing, sweetheart. Come on, I'm taking you home."

"Home?" She blinked, then straightened in her seat. "Oh. All right."

The overwhelming disappointment in her voice had him chuckling. He leaned in and gave her a quick kiss, then murmured, "*My* home, Emily."

"Oh." She smiled, then all but purred, "All right."

The scent of salt air hung heavy in the chilly night air. When Emily shivered, he slid an arm around her shoulders to warm her and she leaned against him as they walked along the pier.

"I like your uncle." Emily spread her hand on Shane's stomach. "He's like a great big, gruff teddy bear."

"Oh God, don't let him hear you say that." But she was right, Shane thought. "He'll sulk for days and probably arm wrestle every male who comes into his pub just to prove he's tough as nails."

"Arm wrestle!" Emily's head snapped up. "Shane, I almost forgot to tell you about Joseph. When I opened my door this morning and he was standing there, I knew who he was."

Shane stopped, looked down at her. "You remembered him?"

"I just knew who he was, that he was my cousin Joseph, and I had an image of him arm wrestling with someone at a family get-together. It's nothing terribly exciting, but it's something."

And that something would certainly lead to more, Shane thought. He felt a moment's fear when he realized that everything Emily remembered would ultimately create more distance between them. Shamed by his selfishness, he touched her cheek and smiled at her. "It's just the beginning, Emily. Before you know it, your memory will come back, either in bits and pieces, or maybe like a floodgate opening. Either way, you will remember.''

"*This* is what I want to remember," she said softly. "Standing here with you, surrounded by the ocean and boats and a brilliant blanket of stars overhead. Eating pastrami sandwiches in your uncle's pub, pasta in my kitchen after making love." She smiled at him. "And whiskey poker."

He grinned, then pulled her closer and kept walking. "Who would have thought you were a cardsharp in your former life? I believe you've been dubbed Whiskey Poker Queen."

"I did do well, didn't I? Though I think they were just being nice and let me win a few times."

"You don't know that crowd if you think they let you win. It's every man and woman for themselves when it comes to whiskey poker. Here we are."

He helped her onto the boat, then held her hand down the companionway. Moonbeams streamed in from the open hatches and small port windows, casting a soft gray light throughout the interior of the boat. He reached for a lamp at the base of the steps, but she touched his arm and stopped him.

"Don't turn it on yet," she whispered. "It's so beautiful down here like this. So peaceful and calm. It's almost like being in a different world."

It *was* like that, Shane agreed. A different world, and with Emily here, that world felt perfect.

A sudden, desperate need to make love to her overwhelmed him. The intensity startled him, made his blood pound in his head, had him dropping his hands from her and stepping back.

"Shane?"

"I want you, Emily." The sound of his own voice, ragged and hoarse, shocked him. "I want to make love to you."

She reached out to him, touched his cheek with her fingertips. Her skin was warm, the texture soft as rose petals. "I want you to make love to me. All day I've thought of nothing else."

He covered her hand with his, pulled her close to him, then caught her mouth with his. She opened to him, met the forceful thrust of his tongue with her own. She rose on her tiptoes, wound her arms around his neck as he deepened the kiss. Passion shimmered and sparked between them like an electric current.

He crushed her to him, slanted his mouth over hers again and again, until a moan rose from deep in her throat. The feel of her breasts, the nub of her hardened nipples against his chest made his heart pound wildly. When she moved against him, rubbed her body sensuously up and down, his blood raced through his veins.

"I need your hands on me," she murmured on a ragged breath. "I think I'll die if you don't touch me, if you aren't inside me soon."

Her words inflamed him, stretched tight the control he barely held on to. He backed her against the galley wall, slid his hands under the ruffled hem of her blouse, then slid upward to cup her breasts. She shivered at his touch, pressed closer to him as his thumbs caressed the pearled tips through the soft silk bra she wore. He found the front clasp and opened it, but could barely tell the difference between warm silk and warm skin as he pushed the sexy undergarment aside to enclose her naked breasts in his palms. On a whimper, her head dropped back against the wall.

And then he bent his head.

An explosion of sensations rocked Emily to the core when Shane clamped his mouth over her aching nipple and sucked tightly. Fire-tipped arrows shot straight to the throbbing at the V of her thighs. How could she bear pleasure this intense? she thought, raking her fingers through his hair, then dragging him closer still. With his rough hands on her skin and his hot mouth on her breast, it was impossible to think, so she simply let herself feel.

When he moved to her other breast and gave it the same torturous pleasure, she thought she couldn't stand it anymore. "Shane, please," she gasped. "Please."

His mouth claimed hers again, and he lifted her, carried her to his bed. She tugged his T-shirt up, and when he pulled away long enough to yank the garment up and over his head, she busied herself by hungrily exploring his hard, muscular chest with her hands and mouth. When she lightly touched her tongue to the tight bud of his nipple, she heard his sharp intake of breath, then felt him shudder with pleasure.

Clothes fell away, were tossed mindlessly aside in urgency. She and Shane fell to the mattress, arms and legs entwined. Tension coiled between her thighs, twisting tighter and tighter. He moved over her, slid his hands up her legs, then spread her knees and slid inside her, fast and hard. Gasping, she reared up to meet him, wrapped herself tightly around him.

They moved together, their breathing labored, their hearts and bodies pounding as one. The tension peaked and broke apart. Her climax hit her like an explosion and she cried out with its force, shuddered over and over and held on tight when he made a deep, guttural sound, then shuddered, too.

She held him, feeling the wild beating of his heart against her and the light sheen of sweat on his body. The light rocking of the boat calmed her, made her smile as she realized this was another first in her life, making love with Shane here on the water.

A wonderful thrilling first, she thought as he brought his mouth to hers and kissed her. She only prayed that this first wouldn't be the last.

Ten

Early the next morning, while Emily still slept, Shane quietly pulled on a pair of jeans and T-shirt, then made his way up the companionway steps to the upper deck. The distant sound of a ship's deep horn cut through the thick blanket of fog that drifted over the water, and the faint hum of a motorboat making its way back from a predawn fishing trip vibrated softly in the crisp, damp air. Seagulls perched on pilings watched and waited, always ready to take off at the first inkling of a handout from an enthusiastic tourist or a softhearted fisherman.

It was a comfortable, uncomplicated way of life. The few other people who lived here kept to themselves, and the weekenders were friendly but preoccupied with taking their own boats out or keeping up with the constant maintenance. Shane had always been content living here. It suited him, he thought. Easy to come and go as he pleased, no one to answer to. No one to worry about.

And then he turned and saw her standing a few feet away, wearing one of his old, blue flannel shirts. The hem cut across the middle of her bare thighs, and unless he missed his guess, she was gloriously naked underneath.

Something shifted in his chest at the sight of her. It wasn't lust, though he certainly felt that, too. It was something else, something unfamiliar. Something that scared the hell out of him.

He could barely breathe from the fleeting moment of panic that gripped him, but when she smiled softly and moved through the lingering morning mist toward him, he forgot everything else but her.

"Morning." Folding her arms, she moved closer.

"Mornin'." He reached for her, kissed her long and hard without a thought to any curious onlookers, then turned her in his arms and wrapped himself around her. "That shirt never looked so good."

"I hope you don't mind," she said sheepishly. "I was a little cold."

He kissed her neck and pulled her back flush with his chest. "I don't think I've ever been jealous of a shirt before."

She laughed softly and leaned her head back against his shoulder. "It's so quiet here, so peaceful. I can understand why you live here, away from all the traffic and chaos of the city. Oh, look, there's a pelican!"

The bird swooped low over the water and was gone

almost as quickly as it had appeared. They were so common here that Shane barely noticed them anymore. But the delight in Emily's voice and the smile on her face settled in his gut like warm cocoa.

He'd never stood here like this with another woman, had certainly never felt like this toward any other woman. He kissed the top of her head, then moved his lips to her temple.

With a sigh, she hooked her hands over the arms he'd wrapped around her. "I had dreams last night."

"If I was in them—" he nuzzled her ear "—it was no dream, sweetheart."

"Not *those* kind of dreams," she said, smiling. "These were definitely dreams, yet they seemed so real. Like tiny bits and pieces of my life."

He stilled, then turned her in his arms and looked down at her and met her eyes. "Is your memory coming back?"

"I don't know. The images were all brief, but still, they felt so familiar to me. Walking up the stairs to my apartment, shopping at a produce market down the street, laughing with Claudia at my kitchen table. They all sort of blended together." She looked past him, stared blindly into the fog swirling around them. "Suddenly I was in a small, dark room. Lights flashed behind me, then I smelled smoke. My heart was racing when I woke up."

Her heart was racing now, Shane realized. He tucked her safely against him, waited a moment until her trembling eased. "Why didn't you wake me?"

"We hadn't been asleep that long and you looked so peaceful." She lifted her gaze to his. "Shane, if I ever do remember what happened that night, I'm going to have to deal with it.''

She meant when he wasn't around, he thought, and felt a stab of irritation that she was making this, making everything, so easy between them. She was keeping her distance.

That was what he wanted, wasn't it? What he'd always wanted in a relationship? Easy, mutually satisfying, but uncomplicated?

Of course it was. That didn't mean he didn't care about her. He cared more than he'd ever allowed himself to care about any other woman. But that sure as hell didn't mean he was looking for anything permanent. When the time came, when her memory did come back fully, she'd slip comfortably back into her world, and so would he.

But the time hadn't come yet, he told himself. He still wanted her, wanted to be with her. He lowered his mouth to hers and gently, leisurely tasted and teased, until she opened to him and met the tip of his tongue with her own. He felt the heat of her body through the thin flannel shirt, the firmness of her breasts against his chest.

It hardly seemed possible that after the night they'd spent together, he could want her so soon, and so desperately. His heart beat like a drum, his pulse raced. His mouth and body molded to hers, and she answered him back with the same urgency.

His hands were sliding down her back, searching for the hem of the shirt, eager to explore the soft, warm flesh underneath, when the screech of a seagull stopped him.

With tremendous effort, he took hold of her shoulders and held her away from him. If not for the heavy fog surrounding them, his neighbors would have gotten one hell of an eyeful. He looked at Emily, saw that her lips were rosy and still moist from his kiss. It took a will of iron not to drag her back to him, neighbors be damned. Instead, he took hold of her hand and pulled her back downstairs.

They didn't make it to his bed. At the bottom of the stairs, he dragged her against him, opened the zipper on his jeans, then reached under the shirt and cupped her bare buttocks in his hands. ''Wrap your legs around me,'' he rasped, lifting her off the floor.

Her arms and legs came around him, and he pressed her back against the wall, holding her with one arm while he shoved his jeans down and entered her quickly. She gasped at his hard, sharp thrust, then moaned and rocked her body to take him in deeper yet.

Blindly, mindlessly, he moved inside the tight, velvet glove of her body. Again and again, he drove himself into her, until they were both gasping, both racing wildly toward the same destination. He buried his face in her neck, felt the low moan rise from deep in her throat, felt her body tighten, then convulse. She cried out, and on a deep, guttural groan, he shuddered, too.

Slowly he eased them both to the floor, then pulled her into his arms. He could feel her heart pounding against his chest, knew his was pounding as furiously against hers. Her warm breath heated his skin when she pressed her lips to his neck.

"You okay?" he managed to say after several long moments. "Did I hurt you?"

She shook her head. "That—" she breathed against his throat "—was incredible."

Relieved, he gathered her close, tucked a strand of hair behind her ear. "You're incredible."

Smiling sweetly, she rose up and pressed a soft kiss to his lips, then nestled back comfortably against his chest. He felt that same grab in his chest he'd experienced up on deck, that same breath-stealing hitch. It wasn't as sharp this time, didn't completely catch him off guard, but it troubled him just the same.

He pushed the uneasiness aside and kissed her forehead. He'd take her sailing today, he decided. Back to the secluded cove where they'd gone before. He'd make love to her there, wade in the cold, salty water and lie naked in the warm sun.

For now, he thought, wrapping his arms around her, it was enough to simply hold her close and wait for the fog to clear.

It felt wonderful to be in love. All the clichés, Emily thought, all the platitudes, were true. The sky *was* bluer, the grass greener, the breeze softer. Every sense was keener, sharper. The tang of peppermint ice cream she'd indulged in a few hours earlier, a baby's laugh from a play yard in the apartment house behind her own, the aroma of cookies baking in a neighbor's oven. Life was like a beautiful kaleidoscope of sights and sounds and smells.

A smile on her lips, she leaned out her open living room window, then called down a greeting to a woman watering the roses in a small garden below. The woman waved, then turned her attention to a bush thick with yellow buds. Emily couldn't wait until every bloom opened. Couldn't wait for the explosion of color and scent.

She backed away from the window and closed it, afraid she might suddenly burst into song.

She glanced at her wristwatch, felt the flutters start in her stomach, even though Shane wouldn't be here for another few minutes. It was foolish, she knew, and most definitely crazy, but love did that to a person. No reason, no logic. Just glorious, incredible feelings.

She knew he cared for her. This past week he'd let down that guard he had always seemed to be on before the night they'd spent together on his boat. Except for the three-day shift he'd pulled, he'd come over every day, stayed every night.

He'd grow restless soon, she was certain, and surely he'd want to move on, but she was determined not to cling. She was equally determined to enjoy every minute they shared, to keep every memory clear and strong.

Someone had told her once that life could change with every breath. She couldn't remember who had told her, but she knew it was absolutely true.

She intended to make every breath count.

The knock at the door made her heart skip. They were going to dinner at Café 88, a birthday party for her mother. Emily had been surprised when Shane had agreed to go with her, especially considering her entire family would be there. She'd seen the hesitation in his eyes—or was it fear?—but then he'd shrugged and said sure, he'd go. Now that it was nearly time for him to pick her up, Emily realized *she* was the one who was nervous.

Her hand shook as she reached for the knob, but the moment she opened the door and their eyes met, her anxiety melted away. And when he smiled at her, when he stepped inside and greeted her with a hungry kiss, her insides melted, as well.

"New dress?" he whispered, skimming his fingertip over the thin strap of her red-print slip dress.

"This old thing? I've had it for ages." Actually, she'd had it for two hours, a last-minute impulse buy from an afternoon shopping trip. Based on the hungry look in Shane's eyes, she was definitely glad she'd bought it.

His fingertip wandered down the narrow strap, then lightly traced the low-cut bodice of her dress. She shivered at his touch, felt her pulse quicken and her knees grow weak.

"If we don't leave now," he murmured, sliding his knuckle over the soft swell of her breast, "we're going to be very late."

With a sigh, he dropped his hand away and stepped back.

She sighed when he took his hand away, then grabbed her sweater and purse. When he turned, she took a moment to appreciate the fit of his black slacks across his firm backside and the ripple of muscle under the long-sleeved blue dress shirt he wore. Good Lord, but the man exuded virility.

Thirty minutes later, when Emily introduced Shane

to her sister at the restaurant, Claudia reaffirmed that opinion.

"A pleasure to finally meet you, Shane." Claudia kissed Emily on the cheek, then smiled at Shane. "I'm happy to see that at least part of the gossip is true."

"Gossip?" Emily slid a nervous glance at Shane. "What gossip?"

"Come buy me a drink while we're waiting for Mom and Dad to get here and I'll tell you."

With a toss of her pretty blond hair, Claudia spun on her high heels and headed for the bar, turning several males heads on her way. An image of her sister suddenly popped into Emily's head: a bikini-clad Claudia lying on a chaise longue by their parents' pool, surrounded by several young men. Daniel's friends, Emily remembered, though she'd only been maybe eleven at the time and hadn't understood why everyone was fussing over Claudia instead of swimming.

Memories like that, little snippets of her life, were appearing to her more often this past week. Though there'd been no significant breakthrough, each time she remembered something she felt as if another piece of a complex jigsaw puzzle had been laid in place. How long, she wondered, before the picture would begin to take shape, or before it would be complete? Would it *ever* be complete?

And did she want it to be?

She felt a strange shiver scurry over her skin. Maybe there were things she was better off not remembering, she thought.

Shane slipped an arm around her shoulders. "Cold?"

She leaned into him and shook her head, let herself enjoy the moment of being with the man she loved in the romantic ambience of this elegant restaurant, with its dark mahogany paneling and crystal votives flickering on white linen tablecloths. Strange that she would feel just as comfortable here, in this formal opulence, as she had at an Irish pub.

They'd barely sat down at the bar and ordered drinks when the opening notes of Mozart's *Eine Kleine Nachtmusik* rang from Claudia's purse and she pulled out her cell phone.

"Frank Gordon, you scoundrel. You've made me chase you all over Boston for a measly five million dollars," Claudia purred into her phone, then covered the receiver and whispered to Emily, "Gotta take this. I'll be back in five, no more than ten."

She blew out of the bar in the direction of the ladies' room, gesturing to emphasize a point, then waving at someone she knew across the room.

Shane glanced at Emily, his brow lifted in question. "Frank Gordon, as in Combyte Communications Frank Gordon?"

"That's the one." The entire world had heard of Frank Gordon, especially since his computer company had been sold recently for around ten billion dollars. "Claudia told me yesterday that he was making a contribution to one of the charities she sponsors."

"A measly five million."

"She's very good at what she does," Emily said

with pride. "My mother told me it's one of the reasons she doesn't work at Baronessa. When she sets her sights on a project, she has a bull-in-a-china-shop personality. The dynamics of working for a large company with lots of family members doesn't suit her."

"But it suited you?"

She reached for the glass of white wine the bartender set in front of her. "Everyone tells me I enjoyed my work. I'm thinking it's time I went back."

Emily's comment hit Shane like a bucket of ice water. With her amnesia, he hadn't considered she'd be going back to work, at least not for a long while.

Or maybe he hadn't wanted to think about it, because he knew that every step she took to regain her life before the accident took her farther away from him.

"You're going back to work?" he asked carefully.

"It's been more than three weeks." She swirled the wine in her glass. "They've set up temporary offices in another warehouse and Derrick wants me to come back to work."

And away from me, Shane thought irritably. Emily's brother had made it more than clear he didn't like her dating anyone out of the Barones' social status. Once Derrick got her back to work and her old routine, he probably thought he'd be able to control her personal life, as well.

And was he any different from Derrick in that respect? Shane wondered. Didn't he want to keep Emily all to himself, too? He wanted to protect her and keep her safe, but without any entanglements or promises.

It was selfish on his part, he knew, and unfair to Emily. "What do you want?"

She glanced up. "What do I want?"

"Forget what Derrick wants," Shane said more sharply than he intended. "Do *you* want to go back to work?"

"I admit the idea of being in an unfamiliar situation with people who are still strangers makes me nervous," she said quietly. "But I need to do something. I need to face my past and think about my future, too."

His hand tightened on his beer glass. "What does that mean?"

"I had a life before my accident, Shane, a family. They will always be my family. Even though I don't remember very much of that life, I know they love me and they'll always be there for me."

"And I won't," he said evenly. "Is that what you're saying?"

She went very still. "Shane, this conversation has nothing to do with you and me."

"Doesn't it?" His gaze met hers and held. "Can you honestly tell me that in the future, as you put it, you could be happy with our relationship the way it is now?"

"I—I wasn't talking about that future. I was talking about working and my family. Why are you saying this to me now?"

God help him, he didn't know why. Still, he couldn't seem to stop it. "Maybe it's the look in your eye when you talk about family and knowing they love you and that they'll always be there. All the things I can't give you. That and so much more.''

"What do you mean, so much more?" She narrowed her eyes. "What more could I want than that?"

"Everything." He had to take a breath so he could get it out smoothly. "Marriage, children. A big house on solid land. You deserve all that."

"Have I asked you for that?" Her words were edged with ice. "Have I asked anything of you?"

She hadn't. And irrational as it was, that bothered him more than anything.

"I'm a grown woman, Shane. I think I know what I want more than anyone else."

"You don't know what you want right now, Emily. When you get your memory back, when you remember who you are and where you come from, everything will be different."

"Who I am and where I come from?" She repeated his words with a cool, deadly calm. "You think if my memory fully returns that who I was will be so different from who I am now? That who my family is and how much money or prestige they have will make a difference as to what I want or don't want?"

"Emily, for God's sake, it's not that simple."

"It *is* that simple, Shane." Her gaze leveled with his. "Do you believe that about me?"

Dammit. How the hell had they gotten to this place? he wondered. But there was no way out now, no turning back. And he wouldn't lie. He couldn't lie.

"Yes."

He saw the hurt in her eyes, heard her sharp intake of breath.

"Emily, dammit, I'm—"

"An idiot," she finished for him, then slid off her bar stool and leaned in close. "A complete idiot."

He took hold of her arm to stop her from walking away, then heard the beep from the pager in his pocket. Swearing, he pulled it out. The code was an emergency call. "I'm sorry," he said tightly. "But I've got to go."

"I understand." She pulled her arm from his hand. "Your family—"

"My family will understand."

Dammit. Of all the times to get a call. He hated leaving her like this, but he had no choice. She stiffened when he moved closer, but did not back away. "We can't leave it like this," he said quietly. "I'll call you later."

"I'd rather you didn't." She rose on her tiptoes and pressed a kiss to his cheek, then stepped back. "Thank you for everything, Shane."

She turned then and melted into the crowd. He took a step after her, then stopped. Seconds could make a difference between life and death on an emergency call.

Maybe it was for the best, he thought as he made his way out of the restaurant. He'd never wanted to hurt her, but he couldn't give her what he knew she wanted, what she deserved.

And still, knowing all that, knowing that it was better to let it end before their relationship got any more complicated, knowing that it was best for Emily, didn't ease the ache in his own chest or the empty hole in his gut.

Eleven

"Three Buds, two pints and a Sam Adams." Katie slid a tray of bussed glasses onto the bar counter. "Table six wants an order of wings and a stack of fries."

While Katie hurried off to bus another table, Shane dumped the tray of dirty glasses, called the food order back to the kitchen, then reached for a fresh round of mugs. With Saturday night Celtics playoffs on the big-screen TV, the pub was packed with fewer families, but lots of thirsty, hungry fans.

"Shane," called Bobby Vickers, a local who worked at the marina yacht club, as he hurried over with two empty bowls. "We need more pretzels, three Coors Light and a pitcher of soda, extra ice."

Bobby turned when an explosion of cheers rocked

the room, then ran back to his table to find out what happened.

"Two Irish coffees, extra whip on one." Katie was back with another order. "One brandy, one hot tea, and the blonde in the corner booth asked me to give you her number."

Shane glanced toward the corner booth, saw the pretty blonde smile at him. He did his best to muster up interest, and was more than annoyed that it simply wasn't there. To be polite, he smiled back at the woman and tucked the slip of paper into his shirt pocket, but he had no plans to call her.

Orders came at him from every direction, but Shane was grateful to be busy. Since his last shift at the fire station, he'd been working at the pub the past three days. It helped keep his mind focused and off other things.

Other things being Emily.

It had been a week since the fiasco at the restaurant. She hadn't answered her phone, though he'd left several messages, and she hadn't returned any of his calls.

It was for the best, he'd told himself a hundred times over the past week. It *was*. He had no reason to feel angry, dammit.

So why the hell did he?

With the basketball game down to the last three minutes and all the customers preoccupied for the moment, Shane grabbed a rag and wiped down the bar, determined not to think about Emily. And he didn't. For all of forty-five seconds.

He cursed himself and the timing of the house fire

that had pulled him away from dinner. He could still hear the cool tone of her voice, could still see the hurt in her eyes and the lift of her shoulders as she'd walked away.

Whatever feelings she'd had for him had been born from gratitude, anyway, he reasoned. Once Emily was back at work and she fully remembered her past, she'd forget about him. Move on with her life.

Find someone else.

The thought was like a fist in his gut. What the hell did he expect? Of course she'd find someone else. She was beautiful, sweet and loving, fun to be with. He'd seen the way other men looked at her, including the guys at the station. She'd have her pick of men.

But just the idea of her being with anyone else had him tightly squeezing the rag in his hand, pretending it was the guy's neck.

"He's doing it again."

Startled, Shane glanced up and saw Katie standing beside his uncle. They were watching him, their arms folded.

"Third time in the past hour." Amusement shone in his uncle's eyes. "He overfilled a pitcher earlier until he was ankle deep in beer."

"I told you," Shane said through clenched teeth. "The valve stuck."

"He put a wedge of lime in Gail Winters's diet cola."

"She liked it that way," Shane defended himself, though he'd clearly made a mistake.

"I suppose Greg Novy liked the cherry you put in his Corona, too?"

Actually, Greg hadn't liked that at all. "So I made a couple of mistakes. Fire me."

"Something tells me you made a mistake, all right." His uncle cocked his head. "But I don't think it has anything to do with working here."

Shane frowned. "What's that supposed to mean?"

"You haven't mentioned Emily for the past week." Katie poured herself a cup of coffee and leaned back against the counter.

"Since when do I ever talk about the women I date?" he said irritably.

"Since when do you bring them to the pub?" Katie remarked.

He never had. But did Katie have to be so damn observant about it? "We were seeing each other for a little while," he said with a shrug, then began wiping down the same section of the bar he'd scrubbed only a moment before. "It was never serious."

"Is that so?" His uncle lifted a brow. "So Emily has nothing to do with the fact that you haven't taken your boat out in a week and you've been hanging around here on your days off?"

"If you don't want my help, say so," Shane grumbled.

The truth was, being alone on his boat only made him think of Emily more. Everywhere he looked he could see her, could still smell the sweet scent of her perfume. And every night he'd reached for her in his sleep, only to wake up and realize she wasn't there. The damn woman was making him crazy.

The knowing look that his uncle and Katie exchanged only increased Shane's insanity. "I'm sure you both have something better to do than worry about my love life.''

''I don't have anything better to do.'' Katie took another sip of her coffee and glanced at Darcy. ''How 'bout you?''

''I've always got plenty of time for a lad with woman troubles,'' Darcy said. ''And for my own nephew, I've got all the time in the world.''

''I've got plenty of time, too,'' Greg said from his bar stool.

''I took my wife flowers when I proposed,'' Henry Cooper said from his stool beside Greg. ''Women like that romantic stuff.''

The pub erupted into raucous cheers as the basketball game finally ended. Shane welcomed the rush at the bar that at least momentarily curtailed any further advice or discussion regarding his personal life.

He didn't need any advice, Shane thought as he filled empty glasses with soda and beer. He wasn't proposing to Emily. He wasn't proposing to anyone.

Even if he *considered* proposing—which he *wasn't*— she wouldn't speak to him now. Not after the way he'd left her.

Whether she knew it or not, he told himself, she was better off without him.

The ballroom of the Ritz-Carlton had never looked more beautiful. Lights twinkled from every corner and the scent of flowers filled the room. Six-foot topiaries covered with blooms of white mums, pink carnations and stargazer daylilies surrounded the outer walls; centerpieces of burgundy roses and bubbling sprays of white baby's breath graced every tabletop. The live music of Benny Goodman and John Coltrane greeted the men and women entering through a red-rose-and-ivy-covered arbor.

Emily stood on the sidelines and watched Claudia personally welcome every guest. Her sister looked gorgeous in the shimmery, strapless blue dress she wore. Diamonds sparkled at her ears and around her neck. Several of the men, in awe of Claudia's beauty, nearly stumbled when she shook their hand or kissed their cheek.

"It's like watching a ballet, isn't it?"

Emily turned at the sound of her mother's voice. "A ballet?"

"The way she moves everyone through, with grace and charm. It's quite captivating. And I do believe that tonight she's outdone herself."

Emily glanced around the ballroom, at the sea of black tuxedos and elegant gowns. White-gloved servers carried silver trays of tasty morsels and crystal flutes of bubbling champagne. "Everything is beautiful."

"It has to be." Sandra snagged two glasses of champagne from a passing tray. "Claudia will be reaching deep into everyone's pockets tonight for the Brookline Emergency Center and she wants to be sure they get their money's worth. Here's to a successful and very lucrative evening."

Emily lifted her glass to her mother's. "I heard one guest ask her if she had a blood bank set up to go along with the two-thousand-dollar-a-plate meal."

Sandra laughed. "Most of the men who've been

dragged here by their wives complain, but once our Claudia turns on the charm, they can't write those checks fast enough. By the way, have I told you how exquisite you look tonight?''

''Three times.'' Emily smiled at her mother. ''But thank you again.''

Claudia had gone shopping with her for the slinky black evening gown that was cut low in the front and high on the sides. In spite of all the compliments, Emily still couldn't help but feel just a little bit like Cinderella at the ball.

Would she ever get used to all this grandeur? she wondered when her mother turned to say hello to one of her bridge friends. Emily knew she'd been raised around money, but she remembered so little about her life. Everyone told her she needed more time, that she shouldn't try to rush anything. She supposed they were right. Time would restore most, if not all, of her memory and help her settle back into a comfortable routine.

But would it heal her broken heart?

Two weeks certainly hadn't eased the pain any. Though she'd smiled and laughed and gone through all the motions since the night at the restaurant, including starting back at her old job, she still felt hollow inside.

Yet, in spite of her pain, there were no regrets. She'd fallen hopelessly in love with Shane, and even though he didn't love her back and was so certain they were too different to have a relationship or a life together, she wouldn't change a thing that had happened to her, including her accident and her amnesia.

Those were the things that had brought him into her life, and for that she would always be thankful.

She forced her mind back to the buzz of conversation around her and a lively rendition of "Boogie Woogie Bugle Boy" that had several couples swing dancing on the floor. She would have a good time tonight, she decided. She would dance and mingle and indulge in the decadent dessert buffet set up in the corner. She already had her eye on a four-layer chocolate cake with whipped cream frosting and raspberry filling.

Sipping her champagne, she turned back toward Claudia, then froze.

Shane.

Looking handsome as the devil in black tie, he stood in the reception line with Captain Griffin and several other firemen from the station. His broad shoulders were stiff, his jaw tight as he moved forward with his crew to say hello to Claudia.

Emily's heart leapt at the sight of him, then she quickly reined her emotions in. He wasn't here for her, she told herself. Claudia had obviously invited the Brookline fire department as her guests, which made sense, since the station worked closely with the emergency center.

But why hadn't Claudia told her? Emily wondered, then narrowed her eyes in annoyance when the answer became clear: because Claudia was working on more than fund-raising here. She was matchmaking.

When Shane stepped up to Claudia, she beamed at him and kissed his cheek. Emily watched as they spoke, then both glanced in her direction.

She'd wring her sister's neck for this, Emily fumed, then quickly turned and made her way through the gathering crowd. She didn't want to see Shane, didn't want to look into his eyes or hear his voice. Didn't want to make a fool out of herself any more than she already had.

She thought she'd managed to lose herself in the throng of people when he suddenly had hold of her elbow. She stiffened at his touch, cursed her sister, then turned to face him.

"Shane." She forced a bright smile. "How nice to see you."

"Really." He led her to the side of the room where there were fewer people. "I suppose that's why you haven't returned any of my phone calls in the past two weeks."

"I've been busy helping Claudia with the fund-raiser." Though she was certain she'd never been a violent person, Emily had an overwhelming urge to kick Shane in his shins. Instead, she held her smile intact. "And of course, you do remember I've gone back to work."

As if he could ever forget that conversation. He'd hated the idea of her going back to work for her brother. He still did, but he knew better than to say so. Though her manner was casual and friendly, the smile on her lips clearly did not reach her eyes, and the stiff set of her shoulders told him she was not quite so aloof as she pretended.

"Emily, I want to talk to you." When she didn't respond, he added quietly, "Please."

He was certain he saw her falter for a moment, but

she quickly recovered and tugged her arm from his hand. "Of course. But this evening is very hectic, and I've promised my time to helping Claudia convince her donors to go that extra mile. Why don't I call you tomorrow?"

Like he'd believe that one. He knew a line when he heard one. God knew he'd tossed around more than his share. "Five minutes. Just give me a chance to—"

"I gave you a chance, Shane," she said evenly. "Now if you'll excuse me, I've committed my time elsewhere."

Chin raised, she turned quickly and walked away. Dammit. He wouldn't let it end like this. He wouldn't. But short of picking her up and carrying her to a more secluded spot, he had no choice. For the moment.

Folding his arms, he stayed on the sidelines and watched her dance with a guy who looked as if he'd sipped from silver spoons his entire life. Smiling and talking, Emily looked completely at ease with the man. When the music changed to a swing tune, the guy went into action. Laughing, Emily followed her partner's intricate moves.

Shane gritted his teeth, swore silently every time the man pulled Emily close. Hell, Shane thought, he could barely manage a waltz without counting.

He watched her dance with two more guys, both smooth, both obviously in the bucks, and his mood grew darker by the minute. He'd lost her. For the first time in his life he'd found the real thing, and he'd lost it.

She'd been right when she'd called him an idiot.

He was heading for the exit when he saw the captain wave at him and the other men who'd been invited to the fund-raiser.

"Party's over," Griff said tightly. "We've got a six-story apartment fire in Chinatown. Three stations have been dispatched and we're closest. We'll meet the trucks there and gear up."

Shane nodded. He hated apartment fires the most. In a large complex, there was a greater risk that someone might not get out in time.

"Let's go." Shane was already tugging his bow tie off.

He didn't hesitate, didn't look back. He did not want his last image of the evening to be of Emily smiling at another man.

Three dances later, Emily escaped the ballroom and headed for the refuge of the ladies' room. Her last dance partner, Ronald, a short, balding man who owned a chain of dry cleaners, had stepped on her toes twice, and the man before him—she couldn't even remember his name—was a corporate lawyer from Cambridge who'd dipped her so suddenly she still had a kink in her neck.

Slipping inside the privacy of the fully enclosed rest room stall, Emily breathed a sigh of relief and lay her forehead against the cool wood.

Her impulse was to stay here for the rest of the night, where she wouldn't have to look at the man who'd broken her heart. But she refused to run like a coward. She'd face the evening, and him, and pretend that all was right with the world, when in fact, it was falling apart around her.

Her skin still burned where he'd touched her elbow. Knowing that she'd see him again when she came back into the ballroom made her knees feel weak. Damn you, Shane Cummings. She pressed a hand to her chest. Damn you.

I can do this, Emily thought. Determined not to cry, she sucked in a deep breath and squared her shoulders. Maybe she'd walk right up to him, talk to him like they were old friends. Surely she could make casual conversation with him, laugh and smile, or—

"Emily?"

At the sound of Claudia's voice from the other side of the stall, Emily took another deep breath but did not respond. She wasn't ready to speak to her sister yet, was still feeling a little betrayed that she had invited Shane here.

"Emily, I know you're in there. Mrs. Larsen told me she saw you go in."

"I—I'll be out in a couple of minutes," Emily said.

"Please open the door," Claudia insisted quietly. "I need to talk to you."

With no other escape, Emily sighed, then straightened her shoulders and opened the door. "I don't want to talk about Shane, Claudia. You have guests you need to see to and we can—"

One look at her sister's face brought Emily up short, made her heart stop. There was more than worry in Claudia's eyes, there was fear.

"What's wrong?" Emily struggled to find her voice. "What's happened?"

"An apartment house in Chinatown caught fire and everyone's been called to fight it. Shane left with the other men a half hour ago."

He'd left? Emily stared blindly at her sister. All this time she'd been out dancing, and she hadn't even known? She felt her stomach twist into a sick knot. "Is...is he all right?" she whispered.

"Come sit down." Claudia was already pulling her toward a chair in the now empty lounge area of the ladies' room.

"No." Emily jerked away. "Tell me what's happened."

Claudia pressed her lips together. "I just got a call from one of the crew. There's been an explosion. Shane and two other firefighters were inside."

Emily started to sway, then grabbed the arm that Claudia offered. Cold dread iced her veins. "Is he...?"

"I don't know any more than that, Em. Come sit down. I'll make a call and—"

Emily drew in a breath to steady herself. "I have to go."

"You're in no condition," Claudia said. "Just let me—"

"I'm going." She was already headed for the door. "I *have* to go."

"I figured you'd say that." Claudia kept in stride with Emily as they ran toward the lobby. "I already asked Mom and Dad to take over for me here and I've called a car to drive us over."

Chinatown was only a few minutes away, but sitting in the back of the limo, with the driver racing to cut the time even shorter, it felt like a lifetime to Emily. Beside her, Claudia held her hand and reassured her, but Emily didn't hear her sister's words. The only sound she heard was of the explosion in the warehouse the night Shane had saved her. Over and over, she heard the blast, saw the rain of brick and fire.

She closed her eyes. Dear God, please let him be all right.

Why hadn't she given him the five minutes he'd asked for earlier? *Five minutes.* Perhaps the last five minutes she would ever spend with him, and she'd been too hurt, too wounded to yield, to listen to what he'd had to say.

She'd never told him she loved him. Her stupid, foolish pride had never let her. Whether he wanted to hear it or not, she prayed for the chance to tell him. He didn't have to love her back, she could live with that. But he *had* to be all right. If he wasn't, she couldn't bear it.

The driver managed to get within one block of the burning apartment before the police stopped the car. Emily threw open the door and ran through the barriers, hearing Claudia calling her, then someone else, a policeman, telling her to stop. But she did not hesitate, did not turn around.

She heard the shouts of firemen as they worked the hoses and trucks and tended to the injured tenants who sat or lay on blankets out of harm's way. Sirens wailed and red lights flashed from the ambulances and emergency vehicles coming and going from the fire scene.

Pushing her way through a crowd of news reporters and cameras, Emily froze at the sight of huge, crackling flames spiraling upward from the two top floors of the structure. Smoke billowed in black clouds from a gaping hole in the fourth floor of the building.

Oh, God, no.

The sob caught in her throat. He can't be in there, she thought frantically. He *can't*.

She heard someone shouting her name, but she couldn't tear her eyes from the flames and smoke.

"Emily!"

Two large hands took hold of her shoulders and shook her. She blinked, then realized it was Shane's partner.

"Emily," Matt shouted over the din of the surrounding chaos. "You shouldn't be here."

"Shane." She clutched Matt's arms. "Is he all right? Is he still inside? Matt, please tell me he got out."

Matt grinned at her. "Everyone got out safe, including Shane. He's a little banged up, but he's going to be fine."

Emily sagged into Matt, relief pouring through her. "Can I see him? Please, Matt, I *need* to see him."

"Come on." He slipped an arm around her waist and led her to a paramedic ambulance on the opposite side of the street. She saw Shane lying on a gurney in the back of the ambulance, covered with soot and dust, wearing an oxygen mask over his face. He lay still, his eyes closed. Breaking away from Matt, Emily leapt inside the vehicle.

"Shane." His name was a strangled cry on her lips.

She knelt beside him and covered his hand with her own. His eyes opened, then focused on her.

Reaching up, he pulled his mask down and frowned. "Emily—" his voice was raspy "—you shouldn't have come here."

"I already got that lecture from Matt, thank you." Her fingers tightened on his. "Are you all right?"

"I'll be fine. Just a little smoke inhalation and one hell of a headache where a two-by-four met the back of my head."

When he started to cough, she frowned at him. "Don't talk."

"Emily, I have to—"

"Be quiet," she demanded fiercely, then pulled his mask back over his mouth and nose. "Now, you just listen and don't say one word."

He lifted a brow, but lay still.

"I thought I lost you," she said raggedly. "All the way over here I kept asking myself what I would do if I never saw you again. How would I ever forgive myself?"

When he started to reach for the mask, she brushed his hand away. "Not one word. Not one. Do you understand?"

He sighed, then nodded.

How could she find the words? she wondered. How could she possibly convey what she was feeling right now? It seemed useless to even try. Blinking back the tears in her eyes, she lifted his hand to her mouth.

"I love you," she whispered. "I never told you, because I knew you didn't want to hear those words. I understand you don't feel the same way, and I know you don't want to hurt me, but it would hurt so much more if you never knew, if I didn't tell you how I feel.''

"Em—"

"Please, just let me get this out.'' She swallowed the lump at the back of her throat. "Whether you like it or not, Shane Cummings, I love you. I know how you feel about marriage, and I can live with that. But I don't know how I'll live without ever seeing you again. If you'll just give me a chance, if we can go back to where we were, I can—''

He pressed his fingers to her mouth, then reached up and pulled the mask down again. "No.''

No? That single word felt like a knife in her heart. She closed her eyes, prayed that her tears would wait until later.

She nodded stiffly. "I—I understand.''

"I don't think you do.'' When she tried to pull her hand away from his, he held on tight. "Emily, open your eyes and look at me.''

She did as he asked, but through the haze of her tears, she couldn't make out his features. He tugged her hand to his chest, then pressed something into her palm. A small box, she realized, then swiped at her eyes to clear her vision.

A velvet box.

"Open it,'' he said quietly.

Her heart stopped when she lifted the lid, then started to race when she saw what was inside: a large perfect diamond flanked by three smaller diamonds on each side.

"It was my mother's.'' He reached for her hand

and slipped it on her finger. "I had it reset with the smaller diamonds on a new band, but if you don't like it, we'll go pick out something together. Or if I'm rushing you, we can just wait a little while, until after you get your memory back. Or if you want to, we— Oh, hell. Will you marry me?"

"What—" She jerked her gaze from the ring, certain she'd heard him wrong. "What did you say?"

"I love you, Emily," he said. "I admit I fought it, but I've loved you from that first night."

"You love me?" Her voice was barely a whisper. "From the first night?"

"It scared the hell out of me." He brought her fingers to his mouth. "But even then, before I knew your name, before I knew anything about you, I loved you. I was going to propose to you at the fund-raiser. I had the ring in my pocket, just waiting until I could get you alone, but then we got the call and I had to leave."

"That's what you wanted five minutes for?" she asked in disbelief. "To propose?"

"I know it's not very romantic," he said with a sigh. "But I wasn't sure when I'd get close to you again where you wouldn't be able to run away."

It was too much to absorb, she thought, too much to even believe. But she looked into his eyes and saw the truth. Saw the love. And her heart soared.

"Shane," she said through the thickness in her throat. "I'll always be a Barone, whether my memory comes back or not. Can you live with that?"

"You were right when you called me an idiot." He pressed a kiss to her hand. "I had to nearly lose you to realize just how big an idiot I am. I don't give a damn who your family is or how much money they have. What matters is that I love you. I want it all, Emily. Children, a house on solid ground, you beside me every night. Just say you'll marry me. God, please marry me.''

''Yes.'' She didn't even try to stop her tears when she leaned down and pressed her lips to his. ''Of course I'll marry you.''

He kissed her, brought his hand to the back of her head and dragged her closer, deepening the kiss.

At the sudden sound of cheers and applause, Emily jerked back. It appeared that several firemen who'd been pulled from duty had congregated around the ambulance. Smiling, Claudia stood with the men, looking perfectly glamorous and completely at ease surrounded by a group of rugged, soot-covered fire-fighters.

''Okay, boys, show's over.'' Claudia winked at Emily, then shut the doors.

And then Shane was pulling her close again, kissing her until she couldn't think, couldn't breathe. When he finally eased his lips from hers, he whispered, ''I love you, Emily Barone.''

''And I love you, Shane Cummings.''

And later, much later, when they lay together in Shane's bed, Emily knew no matter what the past had been, or what the future would be, she was where she was meant to be. Where she would stay.

Always.

*   *   *   *   *

DYNASTIES: THE BARONES

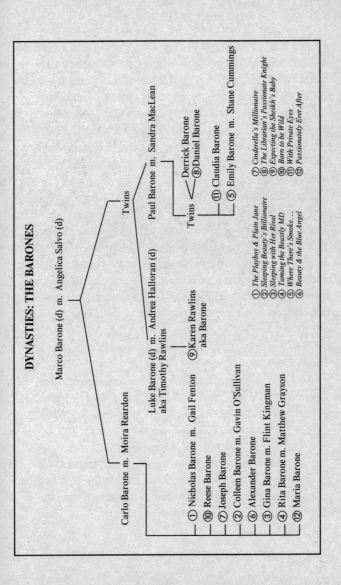

Marco Barone (d) m. Angelica Salvo (d)

Carlo Barone m. Moira Reardon

Luke Barone (d) m. Andrea Halloran (d)
aka Timothy Rawlins

⑨ Karen Rawlins
aka Barone

Twins

Paul Barone m. Sandra MacLean

Derrick Barone
⑧ Daniel Barone

Twins

⑪ Claudia Barone

⑤ Emily Barone m. Shane Cummings

① Nicholas Barone m. Gail Fenton
⑩ Reese Barone
⑦ Joseph Barone
② Colleen Barone m. Gavin O'Sullivan
⑥ Alexander Barone
③ Gina Barone m. Flint Kingman
④ Rita Barone m. Matthew Grayson
⑫ Maria Barone

① The Playboy & Plain Jane
② Sleeping Beauty's Billionaire
③ Sleeping with Her Rival
④ Taming the Beastly MD
⑤ Where There's Smoke…
⑥ Beauty & the Blue Angel
⑦ Cinderella's Millionaire
⑧ The Librarian's Passionate Knight
⑨ Expecting the Sheikh's Baby
⑩ Born to be Wild
⑪ With Private Eyes
⑫ Passionately Ever After

DYNASTIES: THE BARONES
continues…

*Turn the page for a bonus look
at what's in store for you in the
next Barones book*

—only from Silhouette Desire!
BEAUTY & THE BLUE ANGEL (D1514)
by Maureen Child
June 2003

One

Daisy Cusak ignored the ribbon of pain snaking through her. "Just a twinge," she whispered, then ran the flat of her hand across her swollen belly. "Come on, sweetie, don't do this to Mommy, okay?"

The pains had been intermittent all day, but she'd brushed them off. All of the books said there was nothing to worry about until contractions were steady and just a few minutes apart. Well heck. One every hour and a half or so wasn't anything to worry about, right?

Besides, on a busy Friday night, she could make a lot of tip money serving dinner at Antonio's Italian restaurant. And right now, those tips would mean a lot.

All around her, the noise of the kitchen rattled. Pans clashing, chefs cursing, expensive china plates clicking together. It was music of a sort. And the waiters and waitresses were the dancers.

She'd been doing this for four years and she was darn good at it. Okay, so some people wouldn't exactly consider being a waitress a "career." But Daisy didn't have a problem with that. She loved her job. She met new people every night, had a few regulars who would wait an extra half hour just to get seated in her station, and her bosses, the Contis, were just so darn nice to work for.

Rather than fire her for being pregnant, the Conti family was continually urging her to sit down, get off her feet. Someone was always near to help her with the heavier trays and she'd already been assured that her job would be waiting for her after she took some time off with the baby.

"You'll see," she said, smiling down at the mound of her child. "It's going to be great. *We're* going to be great."

"Everything all right, Daisy?"

She turned abruptly and grinned at Joan, one of the other waitresses. "Sure. I'm good."

The other woman looked as though she didn't believe her, and Daisy silently wished she was just a little bit better at lying.

"Why don't you take a break?" Joan said. "I'll cover your tables for you."

"It's okay," Daisy answered firmly, willing not only Joan, but herself, to believe it. "I'm fine. Honest."

Her friend gave her a worried frown, then stacked

two plates of veal parmigiana on her serving tray. "Okay, but I've got my eye on you."

Along with everyone else at Antonio's, Daisy thought. She picked up a pot of coffee, pushed through the Out door and walked into the main dining room. Casual elegance flavored the room. Snowy white linens draped the tables, candles flickered wildly within the crystal hurricane globes and the soft strains of weeping violin music drifted from the overhead speakers.

Above the music came the comfortable murmur of voices, punctuated every once in a while by someone's laughter. Wineglasses clinked, forks and knives clattered against the china, and men and women dressed in starched white shirts and creased black trousers moved through the crowd with choreographed precision.

Daisy smiled at her customers as she offered more coffee and took orders. She bent to grin at a toddler, strapped into his high chair and laughing over the spaghetti he'd rubbed into his hair. Most of the wait staff hated having kids at their stations. It usually meant lost time when the customers left, because the mess left behind had to be totally cleaned before anyone else could be seated. And lost time meant lost money.

But Daisy had always loved kids. Even the messy, cranky ones. Which, Joan had told her too many times to count, made Daisy nuts.

A group of men in their thirties followed the hostess and began to thread their way through the maze of tables to the huge, dark maroon leather booth at the back of Daisy's station. As they passed, she caught a look of apology from the hostess seating them. Four men would be big eaters and probably end up running Daisy's legs off. On the bright side though, they might turn out to be good tippers, too. And she was always trying to beef up the nest egg building ever so slowly in the bank.

Another pain twisted inside her, this time sharply, briefly, in the middle of her back, and Daisy stiffened up in reaction. *Oh, no, honey. Not now.*

As if her baby heard that silent plea, the pain drifted away into nothing more than a slow, nagging ache. And that she could handle.

All she had to do was get through the next couple of hours and she'd be home free.

All he had to do was get through the next couple of hours and he'd be home free. At least, that's what Alex Barone kept telling himself.

He was the last to be seated and caught himself damn near perched on the edge of the leather banquette—as if ready to hit the floor running. When that thought flashed through his mind, he gritted his teeth and eased back on the bench seat. Damned if he'd feel guilty for coming into a restaurant.

Damned if he'd worry about the ramifications.

Although, if he'd known his friends were going to choose Antonio's restaurant, he might have bowed out. No point in going out of his way to antagonize an old family enemy. He glanced around at the place and smiled to himself.

As a Barone, he'd been raised with stories that

made the Conti family sound like demons. But if this was their hell, they'd made a nice place of it. Dim lighting, soft music and scents coming out of the kitchen that nearly made him groan in anticipation.

Nearly every table was full and the wait staff looked busy as ground troops settling in for a big campaign. That thought brought a smile. He'd been in the military too long.

While his friends laughed and talked, Alex let his gaze drift around the room again, keeping a watchful eye out for any loose Contis. But none of them knew Alex personally, and what were the chances he'd be recognized as a Barone? Slim to none.

So he was just going to relax, have dinner, then leave with no one the wiser.

And then in the next instant, all thoughts of leaving raced from his brain.

"Hello, my name is Daisy and I'll be your server tonight."

A gorgeous woman seemed to appear out of nowhere, standing right beside Alex as she gave the whole table a smile wide and bright enough to light up all the shadows in the room.

A purely male instinct had Alex straightening up in his seat for a closer, more thorough look. Her long, curly chestnut hair was caught at the nape of her neck with a slightly tarnished silver barrette. Her eyes weren't quite blue or green, but a tantalizing combination of both. Her pale skin looked satin smooth and soft, her voice held just a hint of humor, and Alex's interest was piqued—until her enormous belly nearly bumped him as she shifted position on what had to be tired feet.

Pregnant.

Taken.

Well, damn. Disappointment shot through him. His gaze dropped automatically to her ring finger, but she wasn't wearing a ring. There wasn't even a white mark to indicate there might have been one there at some point.

He frowned at himself. Not married? What kind of moron would walk away from a woman like this? Especially if she was carrying his child?

"Hello-o-o, Daisy," one of the guys, Mike Hannigan, said on a slow whistle of approval.

Alex shot him a disgusted look, but apparently it didn't bother the woman at all.

"Can I start you out with some drinks? Appetizers?" she asked as she handed around several long menus.

"Beers all around," Nick Santee ordered, and she nodded as she made a note on her order tablet.

"Your phone number?" Tim Hawkins ventured.

She grinned, and the full, megawatt force of that smile hit Alex like a fist to the gut. Damn, this was one potent female, even in her condition.

"Sure," she said, rubbing one hand along her belly. "It's 1-800-*way*-too-pregnant."

Then she turned and walked off to get their drinks. While the guys laughed and kidded Tim about his lousy pickup skills, Alex half turned in his seat to follow her progress through the restaurant. She had a bounce in her step that he liked. The smile on her face wavered only once, when she grimaced, dropped one hand to her belly and seemed almost as if she were comforting the child within.

And who, he wondered, comforted *her?*

As the evening wore on, his interest in her only sharpened. When she brought the pitcher of beer and four glasses, he slid out of the booth to take the heavy tray from her.

"Oh. I'm okay, really."

"Never said you weren't, ma'am."

She looked up at him and he decided that her eyes were more blue than green.

"It's Daisy. Just Daisy."

He nodded, standing there, holding a tray full of drinks and looking down into fathomless eyes that seemed to draw him deeper with every passing second. "I'm Alex."

She licked her lips, pulled in a shuddering breath and let it go again. "Well, thanks for the help…Alex."

"No problem."

He unloaded the beers, handed her back the empty tray and then stood in the aisle watching her walk away.

"Hey, Barone," Nick called, and Alex flinched, hoping no one else had heard his last name.

"What?"

One of the guys laughed.

Nick said, "You gonna sit down and have a beer, or do you want to go on back to the kitchen and help her out there, too?"

Embarrassed to be caught fantasizing about a

pregnant woman, Alex grinned and took his seat. Reaching for his beer, he took a long drink, hoping the icy-cold brew would help stamp out the fires within.

But still, he couldn't help watching her. She should be tired. Yet her energy never seemed to flag. And she was stronger than her fragile build indicated. She lifted heavy trays with ease and kept to such a fast pace, he was pretty sure if she'd been walking in a straight line, she'd have made it to Cleveland by now.

"Geez, Barone," Nick muttered as he leaned in. "Get a grip. There're lots of pretty women in Boston. Do you have to home in on one who's obviously taken?"

"Who's homing in?" Alex countered, but silently reminded himself that she wasn't "taken." At least not by a man who appreciated her enough to marry her. "I'm just—"

"Window-shopping?" Tim asked.

"Close your hole," Mike told him.

Alex glanced around at the men gathered at the table. Men he'd known for years. Like him, navy pilots, they were the guys he'd trained with, studied with and flown with. There was a bond between them that even family couldn't match.

And yet…right now, he wished them all to the Antarctic.

Stupid, but he wanted their waitress to himself.

When she set their check on the edge of the table, Alex picked it up quickly, his fingertips brushing across hers. She drew back fast, almost as if she'd felt the same snap of electricity he had. Which was some kind of weird. She was pregnant, for Pete's sake. Very pregnant. Which should have put her off-limits.

"So, are you guys shipping out now?" Daisy asked, trying to keep her gaze from drifting toward the man sitting so close to her.

His friends were easier to deal with. They were friendly, charming, casually flirtatious. Like most of the navy men she'd waited on at Antonio's. And she'd treated them as she did all of her customers. With polite friendliness and nothing more.

Since the day Jeff had called her a man-trap and walked out the door, leaving behind not only her, but his unborn child, Daisy hadn't given any man a second look. Until tonight. This one man—Alex—with the dark brown eyes and sharp-as-a-razor cheekbones was different. She'd known it the minute he looked at her. And the feeling had only grown over the last hour and a half.

She'd felt his gaze on her most of the night and didn't even want to think about the feelings that dark, steady stare engendered.

Hormones.

That had to be the reason.

Her hormones were out of whack because of the baby.

"No," Alex said, and she steeled herself to meet that gaze head-on. "We're on leave, actually."

"Are you from Boston?" she asked, and told herself she was only being friendly. Just as she would with any other customer. But even she didn't believe it.

There was just something about this man that—

"I was raised here," he was saying.

One of the other men spoke up, but his voice was like a buzz in her ears. All she heard, all she could see was the man watching her through the darkest, warmest eyes she'd ever seen.

"You have...*family* here?"

A slow, wicked smile curved one side of his mouth and her stomach jittered. "Yeah, I come from a big family. I'm the fifth of eight kids."

She dropped one hand to the mound of her belly. "Eight. That must be nice."

"Not when I was a kid," he admitted. "Too many people fighting over the TV and cookies."

Daisy smiled at the mental image of a houseful of children, laughing, happy. Then sadly, she let it go. It was something she'd never known and now her baby, too, would grow up alone.

No. Not alone. Her baby would always have *her*.

His friends eased out of the booth and headed for the front of the restaurant. Alex watched them go, nodded, then reached into his wallet for a few bills. He handed her the money and the check and said, "Keep the change."

"Thanks. I mean—" He was leaving. Probably just as well, she told herself. And yet, she felt oddly reluctant to let him walk away.

"What are you doing in my restaurant?"

Daisy spun around to watch in amazement as Salvatore Conti, her boss, came rushing out of the kitchen, flapping a pristine white dish towel, like some crazed matador looking for a bull.

Silhouette® Desire®

presents

DYNASTIES: THE BARONES

An extraordinary new miniseries featuring the powerful and wealthy Barones of Boston, an elite clan caught in a web of danger, deceit and…desire! Follow the Barones as they overcome a family curse, romantic scandal and corporate sabotage!

Coming June 2003, the sixth title of *Dynasties: The Barones:*

Beauty & the Blue Angel
by Maureen Child
(SD #1514)

Just when single-mom-to-be Daisy Cusak had given up on heroes, navy pilot Alex Barone swooped to her rescue…and captured her heart.

Available at your favorite retail outlet.

Silhouette
Where love comes alive™

Visit Silhouette at www.eHarlequin.com   SDDYNBBA

eHARLEQUIN.com

Sit back, relax and enhance your romance
with our great magazine reading!

- **Sex and Romance!** Like your romance
  hot? Then you'll *love* the sensual reading
  in this area.

- **Quizzes!** Curious about your lovestyle?
  His commitment to you? Get the
  answers here!

- **Romantic Guides and Features!**
  Unravel the mysteries of love with
  informative articles and advice!

- **Fun Games!** Play to your heart's content....

**Plus...romantic recipes,
top ten lists,
Lovescopes...and more!**

**Enjoy our online magazine today—
visit www.eHarlequin.com!**

INTMAG

USA TODAY bestselling author

BEVERLY
BARTON

brings you a brand-new,
longer-length book from her
bestselling series
THE PROTECTORS

Grace Under Fire

She was a Southern beauty with
a killer on her trail. He was the
bodyguard willing to lay his life
on the line for her. Theirs was a
passion like no other.

Available
in June.

Available at your favorite retail outlet.

Silhouette®
Where love comes alive™

Visit Silhouette at www.eHarlequin.com

PSGUF

Silhouette Desire
presents the continuation of

Where Texas society reigns supreme—
and appearances are *everything!*

LONE STAR
L&C
COUNTRY CLUB
EST. 1923

Shameless

(SD #1513)
by

ANN MAJOR

On sale June 2003

A lonely ex-marine
must decide:
Can he snub the
heartbreaking siren
he's sworn to
forget…or
will he give
in to her mind-
blowing seduction…
and a last chance
at love?

*Available at your
favorite retail outlet.*

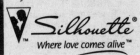
Silhouette®
Where love comes alive™

Visit Silhouette at www.eHarlequin.com

SDLSCCS

COMING NEXT MONTH

#1513 SHAMELESS—Ann Major
Lone Star Country Club
With danger nipping at her heels, Celeste Cavanaugh turned to rancher Phillip Westin, her very capable, very *good-looking* ex. Though Phillip still drove her crazy with his take-charge ways, it wasn't long before he and Celeste were back in each other's arms. But this time Celeste was playing for keeps…and she was shamelessly in love!

#1514 BEAUTY & THE BLUE ANGEL—Maureen Child
Dynasties: The Barones
When soon-to-be-single-mom Daisy Cusack went into labor on the job, help came in the form of sexy navy pilot Alex Barone. Before she knew it, Daisy was in danger of falling for her handsome white knight. Alex was everything she'd dreamed of, but what would happen when his leave ended?

#1515 PRINCESS IN HIS BED—Leanne Banks
The Royal Dumonts
The minute he saw the raven-haired beauty who'd crashed into his barn, rancher Jared McNeil knew he was in trouble. Then Mimi Deerman agreed to work off her debt by caring for his nieces. Jared sensed Mimi had secrets, but playing house with her had undeniable benefits, and Jared soon longed to make their temporary arrangement permanent. Little did he know that his elegant nanny was really a princess in disguise!

#1516 THE GENTRYS: ABBY—Linda Conrad
The Gentrys
Though Comanche Gray Wolf Parker had vowed not to get involved with a woman not chosen by his tribal elders, after green-eyed Abby Gentry saved his life, he was honor-bound to help her. When Abby's brother tried to arrange a marriage for her, Gray suggested a pretend engagement. But the heat they generated was all too real, and Gray was torn between love and duty.

#1517 MAROONED WITH A MILLIONAIRE—Kristi Gold
The Baby Bank
The last thing millionaire recluse Jackson Dunlap wanted was the company of spunky, pregnant Lizzie Matheson. But after he rescued the fun-loving blond enchantress from a hot-air balloon and they wound up stranded on his boat, he found himself utterly defenseless against her many charms. If he didn't know better, he'd say he was falling in love!

#1518 SLEEPING WITH THE PLAYBOY—Julianne MacLean
Sleeping with her client was *not* part of bodyguard Jocelyn MacKenzie's job description, but Donovan Knight was pure temptation. The charismatic millionaire made her feel feminine *and* powerful, but if they were to have a future together, Jocelyn would have to confront her fears and insecurities…and finally lay them to rest.

SDCNM0503